Along
the
Garden Path

Charlotte Strack Peyton

Charlotte Strack Peyton

Feb. 8, 2017

ISBN: 1530089174
ISBN-13: 978-1530089178

Dedication

To all the young journalists and students I have had the honor to teach. You inspire me each day.

Contents

Charlotte Strack Peyton

"Along the Garden Path"
— idiom meaning lead to deception, to be deceived.

1

Racing to Make It

McLean, Virginia
Monday, February 8

Addison wakes to the vibrating and ringing of her alarm and her mother gently shaking her.

"Addison, your alarm's been going off for forty-five minutes. It's already five forty. Please get up."

Addison doesn't even register her mom's irritated and annoyed tone. Now awake, she frantically considers how she's going to get ready for school in time and make her planned stop at Starbucks. She's promised Campbell, her best friend, her favorite chocolate chip frappuccino this morning as a thank-you for helping with her homework yet again. Addison thinks frappes are overly sweet, but so is Campbell, so the choice fits well.

As she searches through the piles of clothing on her floor, Addison thinks of all she has to do. Today's classes are her least favorite, her "odd classes," which means she has Trig. Shoot, the

Trig test she forgot to study for.

She jams her long legs into her dirty jeans, which she picked up from underneath a questionable pile of clothes and papers, and grabs a gray t-shirt before heading to the bathroom. On her way, she texts Campbell: *I'm so sorry, starbucks won't work today! :(Promise to make it up to u...having a slight heart attack...*

Thankfully, Addison is an only child, and a fight for bathroom space isn't something she has to face. She thinks of Campbell and her two sisters, who all have to get to Chain Bridge High at the same time each day. She doesn't understand how the three of them share one tiny bathroom on the top floor. She knows from experience, having spent many nights at the Harpers' home, what those mornings can look like. No wonder Campbell is usually up by four a.m. There's no other way to avoid the chaos.

Addison is grateful that she has a best friend who compliments her personality so well. Without Campbell's support, she'd probably be considering community college. She knows she can always count on Campbell. Not only is Campbell organized and an early riser, she's ahead of her in math and science, so she is always able, and willing, to help Addison prepare. Likewise, Addison's talent is writing and editing, and she has spent several late nights helping Campbell perfect her essays and research papers over the years.

Addison stands in front of the mirror and wonders how she is going to wrestle her caramel colored mane into some sort of hair style. Her green eyes are rimmed with sleep and she decides that at the very least she needs to wash her face with cold water. As Addison is busy brushing her teeth, she hears the ping of a new text: *I got this: meet me in the library at 7. I got starbucks.* Addison thanks God once again for having such an amazing friend.

She quickly rubs some BB cream onto her face and eyeliner onto her lids and decides mascara can wait until she is in her car. She's become masterful at applying mascara at the stop signs on the way to school. She is graced with her mother's skin, so she can get away with the minimal in make-up; her stunning green eyes don't need much in the way of eye shadow, and her features are fine and clean, elegant without being delicate. She grabs one of her favorite sweaters and scarf from the pile of clothing, pulls on tall black leather boots and heads downstairs for a Cliff bar, done within eight minutes.

6:58. Addison pulls into her parking spot at Chain Bridge High School. She curses her spot this morning. It is the furthest parking space in the lot, which would be wonderful at the *end* of the day when she theoretically could be the first who is able to pull out. Only, Addison never gets to leave school early; between track practice and her after-school activities, she practically lives at school.

Chain Bridge High is located in the heart of McLean, Virginia, a first-tier suburb of Washington, D.C. That means two things: Addison's school is only about eight minutes from D.C., so she feels like she is part of the city community; McLean is so close to the "national hub" that most of Addison's classmates' parents are part of the influential system that makes up the government: government contractors, the World Bank, embassies, lawyers, doctors, or own a piece of the housing market which houses the wealthy. In other words, McLean is inhabited by 90 percent type-A, successful, influential, and ambitious residents. Sometimes this is inspirational and motivating to Addison and her peers, and sometimes it is crushingly overwhelming.

She rushes into school, feeling like the local bag lady. She's carrying her track bag, along with her book bag and her lunch. Addison is always worried she is going to forget something she needs, so she errs on the side of caution, and decides to pack anything she might need for the day. This results in her school bag weighing what feels like a hundred pounds. She convinces herself it is part of her weight-training exercises: great for her back muscles as long as she doesn't actually tear them. Her track bag often holds not only her running clothes and shoes but several different weather options, as well as outfits to change into after practice, which causes her track bag to bulge as if it were a mother pig ready to give birth to twenty piglets.

When she gets to the library, Campbell is already waiting for her at a crowded table, with her favorite drink, a skinny cappuccino, Campbell's chocolate chip frappe, and a smile to greet her. Campbell is small and athletic, her dark blonde hair is almost always swept into a hasty ponytail, her bright dark brown eyes betraying her emotions clearly. Campbell is on a travel soccer team, so she's often on the go — to and from practices or tournaments, and Addison has a hard time imagining her in anything other than athletic or comfortable clothing. Today is no exception, Campbell has on a pair of yoga pants and a North Face fleece with a pair of brown UGGS. She hasn't taken the time to put on make-up this morning, but Campbell has an innate beauty, a clean and wholesome look that is only marred by too much make-up.

"Morning lazy... you look like a bag lady, Addie."

"Tell me about it. I wish I could figure out what I didn't need, but I worry that I will forget something important...like my Trig quiz...case in point."

"So, what's the quiz on today? I'll try to help even though it's been a year since I had Trig. Ms. Thompson was a little easier on us than Mr. Hoffman. Jamison was telling me how difficult he is."

The girls sit with their heads together for the next twenty minutes. Campbell's gift for explanation is evident as she clarifies what Mr. Hoffman has managed to muddle in Addison's head in the previous lesson. Why can't teachers simply explain math in words that make sense? They always seem to take the long way around for everything. Sometimes it is as if teachers enjoy hearing themselves talk, making concepts seem more complicated and difficult in order to feel intelligent and important. She wishes they wanted to make it easy for her.

The warning bell rings overhead. The quiet library makes the clanging seem more alarming than in the hallways, and Addison's heart pounds and her stomach sinks as she anticipates her quiz and her dismal grade. Math is so difficult for her; she is clearly more of a language's person than analytical. However, to get into Columbia University in New York City, Addison's dream for the last three years, she knows she needs not only have the math requirements fulfilled, and she needs an "A" each year.

Columbia has been her dream school ever since her freshman year. At the end of the first year of Journalism I, a small group of journalism students and their teacher, Mr. Peterson, traveled to Columbia. It was an exciting experience to travel with a group of students and no mom, and to be in the exhilarating environment of the city made her blood hot. She felt alive in New York City than any other place. With all the people and excitement, Addison felt like she could blend in, go unnoticed. Because she is so tall, a tiny bit over six feet, it is difficult to blend into any group. However, in New York, she felt swallowed up and surrounded by the chaos. Next to homeless entertainers, transvestites, vendors, people of every color and combination, fat people, skinny people, midgets, and giants, her height didn't seem like a big deal anymore. She loves the idea of being able to melt into the environment for a change.

Columbia University, an Ivy League School, is also nationally ranked as the fourth best school in the country, and number one for journalism. That means that there is no room for low grades, missing activities, and being a "member" of a club; she has to be a leader, an athlete, have a distinctive high school resume and stand out in her writing. In other words, it doesn't matter that Mr. Hoffman makes no sense in Trig class; she is going to have to excel anyway. She can't wait for the day that math is a part of her past, not her present or future.

As they pack up their bags, Addison turns to Campbell, "Cams, see you during lunch okay?"

"Good luck, Addie, you got this."

"I'm not so sure Cams. I feel really nervous about it."

As she turns to leave, Addison feels a hand on her elbow. She looks and sees a small wiry boy holding onto her elbow. He looks at her through his small smudged glasses. He is not someone she recognizes.

"I couldn't help but overhear you. I can help you with your quiz."

"Wait? What? How?" Addison looks and sees Campbell has already left the table and is headed to her class.

"I made a little cheat-sheet, it's real simple, you paste it on your water bottle. The teacher will never know. I'm selling them twenty dollars a pop."

Addison hesitates for a moment. It would be so easy to walk into the quiz with the formulas. She could get an A. But Addison hates cheating. She hates liars. She has experienced too much lying in her life and witnessed its ravaging after-effects to even consider cheating. "Um, no, but thanks anyway. I'll risk it on my own." Now she has to consider what to do. She has no idea who the boy is, she has never seen him before. Should she tell Mr. Hoffman? She decides to tackle that problem after her quiz. She wonders if she will see any of these labels on water bottles around her. What will she do if she does? She decides to cross that bridge when she gets there.

Addison wriggles her way through the overcrowded hallways. People are everywhere. She feels shoulders, elbows, hips and feet hitting her from every direction, yet luckily she is tall enough that she can look over the heads of most of the people in the hallway. She can see, far in the distance, the hallway which is her goal, and she maneuvers herself, her school bag and her track bag through the crowd to arrive at the dismal room which is her math class.

Despite Campbell's excellent tutoring and moral support, Addison is still feeling panicky and stressed out. She only has five minutes left to prepare for her quiz. She decides to re-read her notes, hoping that they will make some more sense now that Campbell has brought clarity to her mind. She wonders if she is the only kid at Chain Bridge who won't consider cheating. She can't imagine that Campbell would cheat, but it seems like an epidemic. If this kid approached her so openly, he obviously wasn't too concerned about her reporting him. That tells her he's pretty confident that kids want his help, and that they won't get him into trouble.

As soon as the final bell of the day rings, Addison gathers up her backpack and track gear and rushes to practice. Coach Turner is strict and expects his runners on the field by 2:20. This is a problem today because Addison knows that she should really have stopped by Mr. Hoffman's class to discuss the quiz she took this morning. But the wrath of Coach Turner is enough to hasten Addison to practice, convincing herself that she will visit Mr. Hoffman before school Tuesday...if she can manage to wake up to her alarm.

It is a chilly February afternoon. It always makes her laugh that this is called "indoor track season." Other than the big meets, every practice and meet is outdoors: rain, shine, sleet or snow. Being the mid-Atlantic Virginia climate, one day's practice might bring seventy degrees and sunny weather, and the next day could bring a foot of snow. Luckily, it never stays cold long, and most snowfalls bring snow-days, meaning no school, or practice - and a day of rest.

This is Addison's favorite kind of running weather. The cold air invigorates her. It enters her mouth feeling icy cold and fresh, and she can feel it move through her bronchial tubes of her lungs, bringing fresh, cold air - with it much needed oxygen, into her body. When she exhales the cold air has become warm. Her best running times are always in the winter months; sometimes she wishes the season would last longer in Virginia, where the contrasting summer weather is so imposingly humid, it feels like running through water, breathing the moist air without the benefit of gills.

When Addison gets to practice, as usual, she is one of the first to make it to the track, she starts doing warm up kicks and lunges. She wants to make sure she is prepared for Coach's workout today. They had great results at Friday's meet, but she knows that Wednesday's meet is against their big rival, Yorktown High School. Coach wants to make sure everyone runs their personal record (PR) at this last regular season meet.

"Addison, what's up?" asks Samantha, a teammate and a fellow 800 meter and mile runner. Often, Addison and Samantha run on a relay team together.

"Nothing," focused on her drill, Addison doesn't even look at Samantha. Samantha turns to another teammate to chat while they wait for Coach to start practice.

Addison knows she has annoyed Sam yet again. She can feel the familiar sensation that she should be nice. She wishes she could be like everyone else and relax and enjoy her time, but she cannot shake the need to make the most of every moment at practice, every moment at school. She doesn't understand how other kids can forget about all that needs to be done and needs to be accomplished to achieve their goals.

Addison has been working all season to break the state record and clinch the state title. She is dying to earn a track scholarship to Columbia, in addition to making it into their journalism program. Then hopefully her dad will support her choice. In some ways, she believes that her success as a journalist is linked to her success as a track runner. If she can show her dad that she can leave her mark on track, then maybe he will accept her career choice as a journalist too.

"Runners up!" Coach Turner bellows. "All right, we need to focus on speed this week. I want to see fast starts and even faster finishes. Today's practice will be speed based, so bring your best running to the track. I don't want to see you unfocused, no eyes drifting off, thinking about that girlfriend, or the homework you have to finish. This is *my time*; I am a jealous coach. I don't want to share your mind with anything but my practice for the next two hours!"

As the athletes line up in their groups to receive their directions, Addison overhears two girls gossiping behind her. She gets so irritated with everyone. Why aren't they paying attention? Don't they understand how important it is to be focused and follow directions? Don't they want the team to be successful on Wednesday?

"Guys, shut *up*." Addison whispers, annoyed, to the girls behind her.

"Relax, Addison; it isn't like we haven't done this drill before. Why don't you try to have fun once in a while?" snorts one of the girls.

Addison decides to ignore them. Channel herself into her work-out so that she will know that she has done the best she could in order to make it through the workout, getting the most of her time and effort.

At the end of practice, feeling exhausted, sweaty, but satisfied, Addison stretches along the side of the track. A shadow falls across her, as she looks up she sees a tall, broad, dark-haired boy with big, almond-shaped, brown eyes standing over her.

"You sure were really focused out there, looked like you were preparing yourself for the Olympics."

"Yeah, well I've things to accomplish out here. Sometimes I

feel like I'm the only one with a goal," mutters Addison as she looks around at her teammates, all laughing and relaxing together after the hard workout.

"I'm Mason. I think I know you, I'm a junior too. This is my first year on track...only I don't do any of this running business. I throw shot-put."

"Addison," she says, thrusting a hand out to meet his. "I'm sorry, but I don't think I've met you before. Have you been going to Chain Bridge all three years?"

"Surprisingly, yes. I guess you can disappear in a crowd after all. It makes sense, though, I usually leave right after school, you know to work, and I'm gone every weekend, so it's not too startling that you don't recognize me."

"So you're on track for the first time?"

"Yeah, this is my first season. Like I said, I usually leave right after school, and I am gone during the weekends, so being on a team is kind of pointless. This fall I realized I needed to be on a team for college applications. I want to go to Virginia Tech after I graduate, to study agriculture. I talked to the admissions guy when I visited and he said my chances would be much better if I played a sport, so here I am. I figured with my work experience, shot-put would be the most logical event for me to do. Not much use in trying out for basketball or baseball at this point."

"Well, that makes sense. I'm hoping to get into Columbia University, so I need to hold some records or awards if I want them to consider me; that's why I have the attitude you described before."

"Yup, I haven't seen focus like that in a while. Why Columbia? Isn't that in New York? Last place on earth that I would want to go to school."

"Well, at least you're not shy about how you feel about things," giggled Addison, "I love the city. It brings me to life, I can disappear in the crowds, no one stands out because every type of person walks the streets there. Everyone is on their way somewhere, doing something, following a dream and *living* their lives. Sometimes I feel like the rest of the world is letting life pass them by. Besides, Columbia has the best journalism school in the country, and it's an Ivy League, so even though it's not an acceptable career in my father's eyes, at least the school is Ivy."

"Wow, you have some serious expectations for your life. I'm a simple farm boy," laughs Mason.

"In McLean? Ha. That's a good joke. Where is that farm of yours? Right down Chain Bridge Road? That's a new line."

"I'm dead serious. My parents have a farm out in Marshall, Virginia, about fifty minutes outside of the city. They own a small house in McLean, so I can go to Chain Bridge High and get into Virginia Tech. I wanna run all their farms and grow the business, so I need to study agricultural engineering and business. Yup, I'm a country boy at heart, stuck in suburbia, just trying to graduate and make it to the next step."

Addison looks at Mason with disbelief in her eyes. In McLean, not only are there no farmers, most people wouldn't acknowledge that they know a farmer, let alone that they dream of being a farmer. How did this country boy end up at Chain Bridge High?

"Well, that is a new one, Mason. So, you really like the farmer's life. Why? I would think it's a heck of a lot of work for not so much return, if I've studied my Econ and Finance homework correctly."

"First of all, in Northern Virginia, land is extremely valuable, so having a lot of farmland not too far outside of the city is a great investment. Farming itself, I guess I can't describe it without showing you the farm. The mountains in the distance, the animals that work alongside you, the planting, growing and harvesting food that people are gonna eat. I wanna make my farm sustainable and organic, so it's something that's a bit revolutionary, and it'll help save the earth. It makes me proud and satisfied. Farming has been part of my father's family since they came to this country with the first colonists. I can't imagine doing anything else."

This idea is so foreign to Addison; she can't even imagine how to wrap her brain around the idea. "Well, I respect your passion for farming, even if I don't understand it. I have a passion too, for journalism, which my parents don't understand. I can't describe it other than it is what I think about all the time, and it is all I've wanted to do for years. It is part of who I am."

"I guess we are the lucky ones. Think of all our friends who study either law, banking or medicine because it is what's expected of them, and they know they will become rich in that job."

"You're right. Neither of us will really become rich farming or writing, will we?"

"Not unless we hit the big-time."

"Look, it's been nice chatting, but I need to get home to do my hours and hours of homework. I'm trying to finish a story for the news magazine and I've got to get my editing done as well."

"Gotcha. Have a great night Addison. It was good hanging out and getting to know you."

2

The Birth of a Story

Monday, February 8

When Addison makes it home from practice, she parks her red VW Golf in the driveway next to the garage and the garden gate. The garden surrounds the house and is her mother's pride. In the midst of the garden, her mother's studio sits nestled among the trees, shrubs and plants.

As she approaches the garden, her puppy Chandler greets her from behind the gate. Chandler is a beautiful four-year-old Russian Spaniel, who adores Addison. Because she doesn't have any siblings, Chandler is the closest thing Addison has to one. She often speaks to him as if he were her brother, not a dog. He hears all her concerns and frustrations and listens without judgment. Probably better than a sibling, if she really thinks about it. Each time she comes home from school or practice, he acts as if she is the most important person on earth. Just as he does now, jumping hysterically, so high that his little brown face and white nose peep over the garden gate as she struggles to unlock the latch. When she pushes the gate open, he rolls onto his back instantly, waiting for her to give him a rub, revealing his white and brown speckled little tummy. He kicks pointlessly at something that isn't there as she rubs him under his foreleg. He jumps back onto his legs and wags his tail so much that he can barely keep his body straight. He knows he is not allowed to jump, and it is clear that he is using all his self-restraint not to leap right into her arms.

Addison contemplates what it would be like to be a dog and to have no bigger pleasure in the world than your favorite person entering through the gate.

As she walks through the winding garden path, she considers the fact that she and Mason share the fact that they have unusual families for the Northern Virginia area. Most families in NOVA are moving at thousand miles per hour, with the goal of achievement and drive to make money and more money. Mason's story about his farm gives her a vivid image of him working in the foothills, with the mountains in the distance. She can see him in her mind's eye, big muscles straining as he carries large bags of feed and fertilizer. Growing his own vegetables...she realizes she didn't even ask what he grows, or what kind of animals they raise, but nonetheless, surprising even to her, she likes her vision of him.

She approaches the small structure at the end of the garden path, where her mother's studio sits. In February, only ghosts of the garden exist, the gardenias, daisies, black-eyed-Susans and hydrangeas are all dormant and have been cut back, only the stubs suggesting their impending spring arrival. She can see why her mom likes to come here to create her artwork. It doesn't seem like the studio is placed in a busy suburb of Washington, D.C., but rather a little building in the French countryside. The outer walls of the studio are stucco, the tin roof has turned green with age, and she has window flower boxes, which in the spring and summer overflow with colorful sedge, kale, coral bells, and her favorite, Tuscany violets. Now her mother has placed her dried hydrangeas in the box, accenting them with box-elder branches and little lights, adding a little warmth to the otherwise drab winter weather.

Seeing the garden like this makes her excited for spring to arrive; in a month, the entire garden will begin to transform with crocus, daffodils, and tulips.

She pushes open the green Dutch door of the studio, "Hey, Mom, I'm back!"

Elizabeth Erhard has her back towards her daughter and is sitting in the natural evening light of the open window, working on her newest piece. Black paper is covered with such contrasting images of what one would expect the little idyllic studio to inspire. She is using white charcoal to draw what almost looks like a ghostly image coming out of the paper. Addison often wonders what her mom really thinks in her mind, because the work she creates does not reflect her near-idyllic life in McLean, wife of a wealthy investment banker, mother of a successful daughter, volunteer of the school's PTO and Booster Club. No... these dark and morbid images of chains, figures, angst and frustration don't reflect the person she knows. She wonders who her mother really is deep down inside.

Elizabeth turns to face Addison, her face transforming from concentration to devotion and joy. Her sapphire eyes focus on Addison, appraising her. "Hi, sweetie. You're later than usual! Did Coach keep you to talk about the meet Wednesday?" As she talks, she gets up, wiping the chalk off her hands with a rag. She tidies her materials and runs her fingers through her short blond hair. Her mother is tall, a little shorter than Addison, but is built less athletically; her bones are delicate, with long artist's fingers. Her figure is spare, typical of someone who spends all her time creating, with little time or energy for making or eating meals. Her features are like those she draws: strong, abrupt and stunning. When people pass her mother in public, they always take a second look. When Addison was small, she thought it was because she was tall, but as she has grown up, she realizes that her mother has a rare kind of beauty that comes from deep within her soul, and becomes more impressive the older she gets. Despite being forty-six, she has the juvenility of someone in her thirties, a confidence that is brought on by experience, but a youth which is the results from having joy in doing something she loves.

Addison considers lying to her mom...she really isn't in the mood to suffer through the fifth degree, but she is also really excited to talk about Mason. She can't shake him from her mind.

"Actually, I stayed back talking to Mason."

"Who?"

"He's a boy on our track team. He does shot-put. He and I got to talking. Guess what? He works on his family's farm in Marshall, Virginia, every weekend and all summer."

"Oh, wow, I don't think I've ever heard you mention him

before...shot-put, huh? Is he taller than you? I would think he has to be pretty big to be a good shot-putter." Her mother's knowledge of sports is fairly limited, having grown up in the Midwest, where everyone played hockey or skied. Addison isn't even sure if they had track there. She knows for sure that her mom did not run in high school or college, and therefore, her knowledgeable reference to shot-put throws her off a bit.

"Actually, he is a pretty big guy, but it's his first season playing any sport — I mean any sport at all, so I've no idea if he is any good. He decided he needs a high school team sport to get into Virginia Tech."

"Well, that is extremely unusual for our area. You would expect that he started to practice some sort of sport before nursery school in order to make it into his dream school." Her mother's mockery of McLean is evident. Although she has been a Virginian for most of her adult life, she constantly compares what her childhood in Minneapolis was like, compared to McLean. According to her mother's 80's experience, Minnesotans don't think about college or sports until middle or high school. Addison suspects that even in Minneapolis, little kids are starting sports at a young age, and parents are focused on where their babies will attend college. Addison thinks to herself that maybe that is another story in the making — contrasting college grooming in the Midwest versus the East Coast.

"What does he want to study?"

"Agriculture."

Just as expected, her mom's jaw drops. A farmer in McLean? She can't think of a more unlikely life goal.

"Look, Mom, I have to take a shower, and then we should probably eat. I have a ton of homework to do. What's for dinner?" Luckily, the mention of homework and dinner has distracted her mom.

"I threw some chili together this afternoon. Could you make some cornbread to go with it? I'll pull together a salad too."

Before running upstairs to shower, Addison mixes the cornbread and throws it into the oven. After her dressing and organizing her track bag, she enters the kitchen, as the cornbread finishes baking, indicated by the delicious smell and annoyingly loud timer announcing its end.

She sees that her mom has set the island with two plates. "Dad isn't going to be joining us tonight?"

"It's Monday, honey, you know that all the weekend's business has to be processed. I don't expect him to be back until after seven or so and you know I don't like to eat that late." Addison hears the tension in her mother's voice

"Ok…just double checking mom. No need to be so defensive."

As they sit down to eat, with Chandler devotedly under Addison's chair, they hear the garage door open. Chandler jumps up barking at the unexpected entrance of Addison's father.

"Daddy! You're home early!" Addison is excited for her father to be home for dinner, a rare treat. Her mom doesn't appear to feel the same excitement. Addison tries not to let the problems between her parents affect her relationship with them. She loves them both dearly, and their conflicts hurt her more than she thinks they realize.

Addison gets up quickly to set another place for her father. He puts his briefcase on the bench by the garage door and hangs his coat on the hook in the mudroom, walking in and loosening his tie. At forty-eight, Addison's father is still handsome: he is an imposing man, with a tall, athletic frame, dark neatly cut hair with graying temples. His deep-set green eyes are framed by dark bushy eyebrows, which make him seem more menacing than he is, but the effect is one of power and authority.

He pulls out a chair across from her mom, and greets her coolly, "Good evening Elizabeth, hey Princess." He places a napkin in his lap and they begin their dinner and Chandler places himself under his master's chair.

As her parents discuss their days, and what still needs to be done tonight, Addison's mind is elsewhere. She is thinking about Mason, and herself, and Campbell too. How there are a few kids at Chain Bridge High who do not fit the normal track — the desire to be in a powerful job that will match, or out-achieve, their parents'.

— Well, she did suppose that Mason fit that, since his parents are already farmers, but obviously, by keeping a small place in McLean and having him educated in the best school system in the country,

Fairfax Public Schools, *they* have big dreams for their son, even if he doesn't. Campbell is also unique in that her family is so big that she is expected to bear at least half of the costs of her in-state college education, and Campbell is in the minority for wanting to become a school teacher, not a financially ambitious career to say the least.

Addison contemplates a story idea: what if she writes a story for the news magazine that highlights these types of students? Perhaps there are more kids like herself, those who are hardworking and ambitious, but not because they want fame or money, but because they feel passionate about a career of their own choice. She bets that there are more kids like herself, Campbell and Mason than most people would guess.

"Addie, you seem to be off in another universe, sweetie," says her mom.

"Mom and Dad, now that most of your friends' kids are looking for colleges, or are already sending their kids, what do you think the biggest emphasis seems to be in selecting a university or college program? Or for that matter, choosing high school classes to prepare for the application process?"

"Well, I think most parents want their kids to be better off and experience more success than they themselves have. We want our kids to have even more opportunities. So, for example, I want you to be able to have a vibrant career, and I would like to see you take time to be with your children when, and if, you decide to have a family. I took a small break to stay home with you and focus on being a mom, and although I still worked a few days every week, my focus was on you," her mother answers.

Her father jumps in, "I want a successful career for you too, as an investment banker, I'd like to see you pursue banking or business, or maybe even work for the legislative branch writing banking regulations."

"You guys demonstrate my point well, I have a unique situation: Mom, you're an artist and not a lawyer or doctor, your career is different than many of my friends' moms, so your perspective is a little less rigid. Yet, Dad, you're a banker and your idea of what I should do lines up with what most people in McLean want, money and traditional success."

17

Addison's mom considers her daughter for a moment. "You're probably right. If I think of my friend Marabella, well, she's a doctor and I know she would really like to see at least one of her kids follow in her footsteps and become a doctor. She knows that she has been able to provide for her family, and after her divorce she was able to maintain a similar lifestyle to the one they had with two parents. If I think about it, she has pushed her kids to take classes that would prepare them for a science-based education. Sandra has taken all the sciences offered at school and has also taken classes at Georgetown University at night because Chain Bridge didn't offer them."

"Yeah, I know a lot of my friends' parents make their kids' scheduling decisions and sometimes they end up in classes they hate or miss out on classes that they would love to take. Thank you for letting me choose; I love my journalism and photography classes, even though they won't prepare me for a career following Dad in banking." Addison giggles and her mom joins in. They both realize that her father's dreams of her becoming a banker are naive given her lack of talent in managing her own money. Addie is like her mom; she spends every dime she makes, as soon as she has it in her hand, it's gone. Managing money would be a disastrous career for her.

"Princess, you could learn to manage money, just like you learn anything else in life. You don't have to be a natural at it to be good at it. It helps, but it isn't necessary." Her father is so stubborn at times; it drives her crazy.

"Just like Pops wasn't a natural right? Only he found a way around that, didn't he, Dad? Do you really think that would be worth it? You've spent your life creating an image for the company that is honest and reliable. The last thing you need is for me to come in and make a mess of things."

"Addison!" both her parents yell at once. Clearly she stepped over the imaginary line. Time to pretend the Erhards are perfect. At least her parents are united on that front.

"Never mind. Forget I said anything. The point is, do you think that would make a good story for the news magazine? Discovering how many kids don't plan on following their parents' footsteps and then interviewing a few kids who are following their parents' plans with excitement. I'm sure those kids exist as well."

"Addie, I think it would make a great story, and I think it is relevant and should be told. So many people in this area get absorbed into 'the plan' and they lose track of what they really want in life. I've seen many wealthy and successful people who are lonely and sad. I often think the trade-off is not worth it."

"Thanks, mom, I'll see if I can get some interviews tomorrow. I'm going to head up to do homework. 'Night Mom, 'night Dad, try not to kill each other, okay?"

"Good night, sweet girl. I'll come check on you before I head to bed. I want to work on my drawing a little more before I turn in."

Addison gathers up her plate and cup, and places them in the dishwasher, Chandler following her as she moves about the kitchen. As she wanders up the kitchen stairs, which run along the back of the house and directly to her bedroom, she contemplates the pieces of her story.

Addison curls up with Chandler on her bed and gets her phone out to text Campbell. Her room is her retreat from the world, and she loves it. She has a comfortable queen bed, positioned cozily in the corner, coming out at an angle from the far corner of her room. She likes this position because she feels like the bed is the center of her room. Her bed faces her cozy window seat, which is nestled in a bay window along the south wall and overlooks her mother's garden. It's a big roomy seat with fluffy cushions. She shares her mother's taste and loves the French Country toiles in pinks and yellows. She has a variety of fabric on her pillows and drapes. She spends hours in this seat studying and reading, and she has come up with her best story ideas here, gazing into the garden.

Her bed is similarly piled high with extra cushions, and she loves to snuggle between them and her sweet Chandler. Her father has given her the antique furniture that belonged to her grandmother. She never knew her grandmother, because she passed away before her parents were even married. Having her grandmother's furniture makes Addison feel like she's got a part of her grandmother with her always. The furniture smells of roses and cherries with that mustiness of antiques, which isn't quite the smell of mildew or offensive, but a mustiness that speaks to the furniture's history and has its own story to tell. When she opens her drawers, she wonders what her grandmother was like at her age...did she want to become something grand? Was she in love with a boy? Was she dreaming of traveling the world? Did she hide secret letters at the bottom of these same drawers?

She moves her train of thought from her grandmother to her text to Campbell.

Hey Cams...I met a boy.

A few seconds later, Addison's phone pings.

Like a real-live boy? ill believe it when I see it.

Hes huge. like he makes me feel tiny.

Does this boy have a name?

Mason.

As in Mason Gentry?

You know him?

Hottie. duh. seriously. you live under a rock

Well.now I know hes cute.

Are you going to ask him out?

No...that would be terrifying. I have a plan tho

What is it?

Wait and see....TTYL

She puts her phone away and forces herself to focus on her article. She needs to research her story idea. She needs to know if the kids at Chain Bridge High achieve more, dream bigger and put more pressure on themselves than students at the average American school. Then she needs to find the outliers, those students whose dreams and aspirations don't line up with the 'norm,' if there is such a thing. Is this reputation that Chain Bridge High has of high-achieving, overly-driven students and athletes really legitimate, or is there another story here?

Addison taps her laptop awake, and as she does so, she scratches Chandler under his chin and behind his ears. He stretches out lazily and looks at her in total contentment.

"Chandler, what must it be like to be a fabulous Russian

Spaniel with every need met, and where a scratch along the ears makes your day? No stress, no worries."

He looks up at her with his big brown eyes as if she doesn't get it. Hasn't she seen him lose his mind over the rabbits in the garden, or when someone arrives at the door unannounced, he seems to say. She giggles to herself and realizes that everyone and all creatures have their own stresses. Just varying levels of stress, but to that person, or in this case that dog, that stress is real in that moment.

Her computer is humming and ready. She opens Google Chrome and begins searching. The first question she wants to answer is whether the number of kids who graduate, and go to college after school, is the same at CBHS as other schools in Virginia and in the nation. Then she wants to see whether McLean kids actually go to better universities than the other schools in the district and in surrounding districts.

She types Chain Bridge High School graduates into Google and finds a Fairfax County website with data about last year's graduation rates. Ninety-six percent of CBHS graduates attend colleges. Okay. That sounds perfectly normal to Addison. She can't imagine a student who wouldn't want to go to college, or wasn't planning on it. She can't think of a single friend of hers who isn't planning on attending college after they graduate.

She looks up college attendance rates nationally. She finds that the average rate of high school graduates attending college in Virginia is sixty-four percent, the highest state attendance is Connecticut with seventy-eight percent. The lowest attendance state is Alaska, with a mere forty-eight percent of graduates attending college. Well, that certainly makes ninety-six percent seem extraordinarily high. She mulls this over; it is so foreign she can't imagine it. She thinks about the types of jobs someone could get right out of high school. She imagines she could probably start writing freelance, but also supposes she could earn more money writing with a degree and some experience. There are landscapers, garbage men and women, postal workers, store clerks, butchers, bakers, gardeners...the more she thinks about it, the more she realizes that there are many jobs people could start right out of high school, where on-the-job training is the education. Obviously, the country wouldn't be able to run without these people. It's crazy to her that she is seventeen and for the first time is considering what life would be like if she weren't growing up in an area with an expectation that everyone should not only graduate and go to college but is expected to go to an excellent college and have a successful career.

So, how many kids actually go to a "good college," i.e., an Ivy League, or a first-tier college? She Googles Chain Bridge High School college attendance and finds an article by the McLean Patch. The story states that students who graduated last year from CBHS attended all the Ivy Leagues, in addition to three of the military academies, including the Coast Guard Academy, which was listed as the first ranked academy. A multitude of accepted CBHS students played sports at those schools as well. In addition to the Ivy Leagues, schools attended were prestigious schools such as Duke, Notre Dame, Tulane, Oberlin, Stanford, MIT, and CalTech. The article also went on to say that those students who didn't make the list of Ivy Leagues and distinguished schools were getting accepted at competitive state schools, such the University of Virginia and The College of William and Mary.

The more Addison researches, the more impressed she is by her own school. She finds that *U.S. News and World Report* has ranked Chain Bridge High in the top five Virginia schools in the last decade, and in the top thirty in the nation.

So, are CBHS kids actually more successful than their graduating peers from other area schools? A quick search of "famous CBHS graduates" brings up a list of success stories, including screenwriters, mathematicians, Nobel Prize Laureates, famous opera singers, politicians, economists, novelists, and astronauts. It would appear that, indeed, attending Chain Bridge would increase the odds for a successful future. The question is, how much pressure are students and parents putting on themselves and their children to achieve more and better than the previous generation? The expectations that Addison has put on herself, and what she sees her friends and peers put themselves under, is overwhelming. She wonders if it is worth it.

She thinks again of Mason, who seems to have set himself apart from the machine. He wants to become a farmer, he wants to study agriculture at a "good" school, but not the best school. He hasn't played sports until this moment because he hasn't felt the need to. All those practices that Addison has attended, soccer, softball, track, all to prepare her for a potential sports career in order to get into the best college possible, they seem futile. How did Mason escape all that? Obviously, his parents are successful, they own valuable country land, but they also own a home in McLean that they keep for the purpose of having Mason attend the best high school that he can. She wonders if his parents actually want more for him than he does, if they dream of Mason attending an Ivy League. Are they disappointed with his choice to follow in their footsteps?

She also thinks of Campbell Harper, who is growing up in a unique-to-McLean environment, with a large family, in a small house, with no trust fund to get her through school. She knows that Campbell wants to become a teacher, also not your typical McLean career. But she loves kids, and as the oldest in her family of seven, Campbell has had lots of opportunities to teach little ones. She also doesn't seem to feel the same pressure as her peers. Maybe it's her family dynamic, or maybe like Mason, there is a drive to do what she loves, regardless of whether it makes her a 'success' or brings power and prestige.

Addison thinks about the angle of her story. How is she going to pull off this alternative attitude without it backfiring? What does she want the reader to walk away with? As a journalist, she has the power to influence the way people think. Maybe her article will make other students consider what really matters to them. Are they following careers as doctors, lawyers, politicians and bankers because they want power, or because they love it? Maybe some of her readers will consider changing their minds and pursue their passion instead of society's expectation.

Or, they could mock her and her story, and tease the kids she interviews, those who choose to follow their dreams. That would be disastrous, and she would put her interviewees in a horrible place. She knows she has to write this story, and she knows she has to make sure it highlights the positive aspects of following the heart and a person's dreams. As she closes her laptop she formulates the story in her mind and gets ready for bed; she knows this has to be the best article she has written to date.

Addison pads into the bathroom and begins her night time ritual. She brushes her teeth while doing squats, she washes her face with her favorite soap from Lush and lathers on face cream. As she brushes her long, thick hair, she walks back into her room to find her mother sitting on her bed.

"Hey mom, what's up? I'm getting ready for bed."

"Hey, sweetie. I think it's time I tell you a little story about your dad, me and your Pop.

3
Like a Thief in the Night
May 13, 1998

"I'm going to tell you a story tonight that I hope will help you understand what Pop did, and why your father and I don't always agree.

"I don't understand, Derrick." I couldn't believe he dropped this bombshell on me, days before our wedding. Derrick stood facing me in my small apartment in Dupont Circle, near the windows that overlook Massachusetts Avenue in Washington, D.C., as the rain poured down from the heavens outside, in thick sheets of gray. It was May 13, 1998, and we were to be married on Saturday, May 16, at St. John's Episcopal Church in McLean, Virginia, the prestigious and affluent suburb of Washington where Derrick grew up and where generations of his family lived.

"I've discovered that Pop has been hiding money from his clients." I looked at my fiancé's strong features; he was worn-out and tired, making him look much older than his thirty years. His dark, deep-set blue eyes were clouded with worry. He ran his strong hands through his dark hair. His height and strength were diminished by his anxiety.

"How did you find out?" I asked in disbelief. Derrick's father owned a successful investment firm in the city; he put his entire life into the firm, building the family legacy. Derrick was set to take over operations of the firm by taking over as Vice President as soon as we returned from our honeymoon. Derrick's

father, Derrick Ronald Erhard, Jr., affectionately known as JR by his friends and family, had been grooming his son for this, first sending him to Boston College for his undergraduate in business administration and finance, and then off to The University of Pennsylvania for an MBA and Masters in Finance. My Derrick, or Trip, as his family called him, was poised to take over the business, but what I was hearing now was that the firm was not as we had expected it to be.

"It's a mess, Lizzy, a huge mess. I'm so disappointed in my father."

"Okay, calm down, baby." I circled behind him and wrapped my arms around him, nestling my head between his shoulder blades. Derrick was a powerful man who had run track in college, and he maintained his physique by running regularly. It didn't matter if it was rain or shine, he was out running. I could feel the muscles under his light cotton shirt. "I know we can work through this. It shouldn't affect our wedding. You know I would be with you no matter what. It's never mattered to me if you're a successful banker or a poor gardener. As long as we share a home, a bed, and our love. I can face anything as long as you are by my side."

Derrick turned around so that he was facing me, and he cupped my face in his hands. "Your words mean the world to me. It's what I love best about you, the fact that you take me as I am. Through sickness and health, right?" His eyes bored into mine. They searched as if trying to see if there was a hidden message that he was missing.

"I mean it, Love. We could be living in an efficiency in New York, as long as we have enough money for canvases and ramen noodles, I will be content." I meant it. His money had been more of a deterrent to me than an attraction. I didn't want to spend my life feeling obligated to him, his family and their money. I would have preferred to marry a simple man, knowing that we owed only ourselves for our successes and failures. But I learned early on, after losing myself in Derrick's deep emerald eyes and spending long nights talking and discussing the world and what we wanted, that I could not fight my attraction to him. I could not help but accept his money, his drive, and his family and all that entailed.

Yet, here we stood at the precipice of marriage and our future. Upon our return from Italy, we would move into the enormous house in McLean. To me it was a mansion, even though I knew that technically, it was missing the ballroom and servants a mansion would necessitate. The house could have fit five of my parents' homes in it. I knew it would be a challenge for me to create a space in the vast structure that would feel like mine, a place to feel at home in.

From what Derrick was telling me, we were at risk of not following this well laid path we had planned.

"So, explain to me what's going on." As I said this, I poured two big glasses of Malbec, Derrick's favorite. I handed him one and took his free hand in mine and led him to the small sitting area. We sat next to each other on the antique sofa I had rescued from my grandmother's home when she moved into the care facility a few years before. Knees touching and facing one another, Derrick began to tell me what he had uncovered.

"Okay." He took a deep breath; I could see he was gaining the courage to tell me the entire story. "A few months back I was going through the account books, I wanted to be sure that everything is in order before I take over. Pop seemed to be in such a rush to hand it all over, something didn't sit right. He said he wanted to give us a good start to our marriage, but it felt like he is trying to push it off, rushing through it. The way I see it, either he really wants to retire and move to the South, or something else is going on. I've caught him avoiding answers and making up little white lies too."

"What kind of white lies?"

"I'll say, 'Father, where is that paperwork for so-and-so'...only he can't find it, and he blows it off, blaming his assistant for misplacing it. Then, when I remind him later, he pretends he doesn't remember that I ever asked. You know how he can be gruff and dismissive? He does it all the time at work - to me, and it wasn't always like that." I looked at Derrick more carefully, his hands were trembling, his eyes looked bloodshot. I could understand the late nights now. The extra glass of wine or shot of bourbon after dinner. I could see that all this was taking its toll on him. Anger bubbled up inside of me. Not only was JR doing something with his firm, his actions were having a grave effect on my fiance.

"So, you think he is hiding something?" I asked hesitantly.

"I do, I have a gut feeling, and I'm terrified to find out the depth of it."

"Do you have any idea what it could be, and what the implications are?"

"Yes, I do. The reason I'm so upset today is that I think I found incriminating evidence."

"What?" I gasped, covering my mouth with my hand, terrified to find out what had disturbed my otherwise immovable Derrick.

"I found a transfer from one of our client accounts to another client's, without any correspondence from them indicating they wanted the transfer. When I dug a little deeper, I found that same sum transferred to several different accounts, until I found it in an off-shore account."

"*Derrick, am I understanding you correctly that you suspect that your father has embezzled client money into some sort of off-shore account?*"

"*That is exactly what I am fearful of.*"

"*Oh, God. What will you do?*"

"*Well, I can make that money re-appear if Father comes clean with me. God knows, if he's doing it now, who knows how long these things have been going on. He could have embezzled any amount of money from his clients - clients he's been working with for ages, clients who have trusted him. I don't even know where to begin in confronting him, having him come clean, and then putting things back in order. But it has to be done, I can't work in a corrupt business; I will not look the other way. I know that in this business, and in this day and age, people are corrupt, hell, it's nearly the expected: they do unethical things. I can't sell my soul like that.*"

"*Derrick, are you going to report this to the authorities?*" My words were intended more as a rhetorical question than an authentic one. The answer seemed obvious to me.

"*No!*" Derrick got up and walked away from me, looking out of the window over Massachusetts Avenue. I could see the conflict brewing inside of him. "*I can't do that for many reasons. Father would serve time, the company would be destroyed, and if it somehow were to survive, then rebuilding our reputation would take decades. We would lose everything, Lizzy. My career as an investment broker would be finished. I share not only his name, but his reputation as well. Years of schooling, years of grooming myself, building relationships of trust with clients. All up in smoke.*"

"*But you can't let him get away with it! He has stolen money from his clients. How can you turn the other way?*" Now I stood up, coming closer to him, but keeping my distance. I was revolted by what he was telling me.

"*I wouldn't turn the other way, not completely at least. I would make Father leave the business. He has to retire immediately. I'll return the funds, and find some way to explain it to the clients so that they don't believe it was Father embezzling. Then, I'll work very, very hard to make sure everything that happens in that office is clean, tracked, and transparent. I want people to know when they trust us with their money, it is safe.*"

Derrick passionately defended himself. He made it seem as if hiding these crimes was the right thing to do. I believe he had already convinced himself that by handling it on his own, he would undo what JR had done. Only, it didn't sit right with me. How could I stand by when the law was broken? People's money had been taken for personal gain and hidden in some off-shore account. I didn't *think I could enjoy our planned future: the house, the cars and jewelry purchased with that money. It would be tainted by what his father had done for God knows how long.*

"Derrick, I don't know if I can stand by, live in that house, off that money. It goes against everything I am, everything I know."

"Lizzy, please listen to me. I attended six years of school, I have spent every summer and vacation working for Father while all my classmates spent their time at the beach or on vacations in Europe. I have put years of work into the firm. I'm confident that the work I have done has been honest. I know that the people who work for Father have earned their money, they support their families, and they are good people. If the company implodes, not only do I lose everything that I have been working for, but all the employees do too, and they will be equally tainted with the shame of Father's guilt. No one will hire them knowing that they may have taken part in this."

"But, Derrick, maybe they did! How can you trust anyone who worked for your father?" Exasperated, I stormed across the small room into the kitchen, where I refilled my wine glass.

"I will have to spend many, many late nights cleaning things up and finding out if anyone other than Father knew about this. I will remove anyone who was associated with it, but I will not punish innocent and hardworking employees for my father's greed."

I knew that he had many good points, but my gut sickened at the thought of letting JR go without punishment. He had always seemed like a slippery snake to me. He always said the right things to everyone, pulling everyone into his trap through flattery and feigned interest. Except my parents. He clearly had little respect for my Minnesotan parents; he wasn't impressed with my dad being a professor and my mother a housewife. His interest in those with power and money always seemed so transparent to me. But I adored his son. Derrick was everything his father was not. Yes, he had money, but he understood the value of working for that, for respecting people, regardless of where they came from. He treated my family just as well as he treated those clients and friends who were worth millions. I often wondered what his mother had been like; she must have been incredible to raise an incredible person like Derrick. It was unfortunate that she died young; and that I never got to meet her.

I looked up at Derrick, who stood before me with pain in those green eyes and hope etched in his features. "Derrick, you know I love you more than anything, but I need to think on this. It changes everything for me."

"Lizzy, what are you saying? Elizabeth?" His sweet face was crestfallen;

29

I could tell he never anticipated that I would hesitate to accept his solution. He believed so strongly that he could handle it and administer justice himself.

"My sweet, sweet man, I know your heart is in the right place, but I don't know if I can live my whole life knowing that we aided a criminal, that we did not do right by the law."

"I guess you need time to think then. I am not going to sacrifice what the Erhards have worked to build for generations because one corrupt man became greedy in his old age. I can't do that."

My heart shattered into a thousand pieces at his words. How could I choose? I wished he could see it from my perspective. If I were willing to live with the simple things in life, why couldn't he? Wasn't I enough for him? Why did he need the bank, the house, the money and the legacy? He has so many other talents that he never acknowledged. He was incredible at gaining the trust of those around him, of managing people. Somehow, we would manage, I knew that we could. If only he could have as much faith in himself, in us, as I did.

He got up and gathered his coat, preparing to be enveloped by the storm raging outside, and within himself. His face reflected the emotions I felt. Distress, heartbreak and conviction. Just as I was convinced that I knew what was right, so was he. It was the characteristic I loved so much about him.

Elizabeth turns to Addison, having told this family secret for the first time in its entirety. She looks at her strong daughter, who holds the same strength of character as both her parents. The conviction of knowing what is right and wrong, and the strength to carry out those beliefs. Her caramel-colored hair frames her face. Her clear green eyes hold the same clarity that once drew Elizabeth to Derrick. It is hard to imagine that eighteen years have passed since that May day. They sit together on Addison's window seat in her cozy bedroom overlooking the garden and studio Elizabeth loves so much. The same house that so long ago she couldn't imagine living in.

"I always knew that something had happened with Pop and the firm, and I knew that Dad had worked hard to correct it, but I didn't realize that Pop had been stealing money for all those years. Wow. Why did you decide to accept Dad's solution?"

"It's really simple in the end. I loved him. I loved him more. than anything. The panic I felt when he walked out that door. It was crushing. It was then that I realized that just as I could live somewhere with nothing but to be with your dad, I could live with this too. I needed your dad to be complete. Without him I was just a part of myself, but not the whole."

"But, did you ever really accept it?" Addison looks at her mother with the innocence that only youth can deliver. The belief that you can stand by your ideals, your convictions and do what's right, without question. She gazes at her with the hope that her mother will uphold this naive belief. Hoping that her mother did not have to sell out to love her father.

"No, I struggle every day with that decision. Every purchase I make, each time I come home, I can't help but think that we don't deserve any of it. So, I hide myself in the only place that was built by my money, my studio; I feel at home there, and at peace."

"I'm glad you told me mom, I am glad that you trust me enough to tell me the truth."

"I know it's a lot to digest, and I don't really expect you to understand completely until someday you love someone they way I loved your dad."

"Do you still love him like that, Mom?" Again, Addison's face shows its trust in true love, the innocence and hope of the young.

"I'll always love your dad, but that doesn't mean it is easy to forget or to accept. Ok, Addie, sweetie, I have kept you way past your bedtime with my story. You have to get to sleep. Know that I love you more than I've ever loved anything in this world, and you wouldn't be you if you weren't like your father." She kisses her daughter on her forehead and quietly walks out the bedroom; leaving Addison with both the relief of the truth, and its burden.

4
The Newsroom

Tuesday, February 9

On Tuesday morning, Addison gets to school early so that she can talk to Mr. Peterson before the warning bell. She wants to run her story idea by him before she invests too much time researching and preparing interview questions.

As is typical for Mr. Peterson, he is in his classroom early, and the room is full of students who either want to talk with him, or just want a place to hang out before school begins. There is always a busy buzz in the journalism room; between rushing to get stories written, edited and published, someone is always in a panic or a rush to make a deadline.

This is a mid-cycle day. The staff has already sent out the February edition for publishing, so they are in the writing phase of the March news magazine. Students are writing articles about a wide variety of topics and the editorial staff, made up of ten students, is busy reading stories on the Google drive and leaving feedback for the writers. The editors have read all the pitching forms and will meet to decide what they want to highlight in this month's edition. Addison plans to persuade her staff that they should run her story as the cover story.

As Co-Editor-in-Chief of the magazine, Addison has some seniority over other editors, and if all goes as planned, she will be Editor-in-Chief during her senior year. Another huge plus for her application to Columbia. This also means that she has to read and edit all the stories along with the Editor-in-Chief, William Davis.

Sometimes it feels like her editing and managing of the publication takes away from what she really loves to do, which is to write.

As it happens, William is already in the journalism room when she arrives. William is compactly built, making his five-foot-five-inch frame seem much larger than it really is. His cafe au lait skin contrasts dramatically with his green eyes, revealing his parentage of mixed race. William has an extremely serious persona, working efficiently whenever in the class, and often sending out reminder messages and clarification messages during the evenings and weekends. In other words, he is a highly effective Editor-in-Chief.

"Hey, William! Good morning Mr. Peterson."

"Well, good morning to you. What brings you to school this early, Miss Erhard?" Mr. Peterson is large and burly. He is perhaps in his mid-forties. He has shaved his head, and is generally an imposing figure, with a stature well over six feet, and broad shoulders. He normally wears his journalism teacher uniform, which seems to be a little more relaxed than other teachers, a polo with khakis. Addison thinks he has a polo in every color of the rainbow, plus some.

"I'm actually here to pitch a story idea to you, so I'm really happy that William is here too. I think this could be our cover story."

"What is it?" asks William. "I've already seen some really strong stories we could run."

"You know that Chain Bridge High School has a reputation in the area for being stuck-up snobby kids who all become doctors, lawyers, bankers or politicians, right?"

"Well, I'm not sure I agree with that description, Addison," Mr. Peterson looks over his reading glasses at Addison. Clearly she had pricked some sensitive area here. Good. This is the response she wants to see.

"Exactly. Now that I'm seriously considering where to go to school and what I want to study, I've been asking my friends, and other people I meet what they want to study and where they want to go. What if I write a story about students who have a unique vision and plan for their future? I'm sure there is someone who wants to work for the Peace Corps, or become a doctor who works with Doctors Without Borders. Maybe there is some crazy fool who wants to become a journalist..." Addison looks over at William, and winks at him; they have both discussed whether being a journalist is a viable career in the digital age, and William isn't convinced yet. "Maybe some kid out there wants to become a farmer, or a forester."

"That is an interesting angle, but what is your main point of the story?" asks Mr. Peterson.

"I want to show our school and community what a diverse and unique student body we have, in an attempt to dilute this idea that we are all a uniform student body with the same goals."

"Be careful, because you are going to run into those kids who are the 'stereotypical' kids, so you want to make sure you don't alienate them. You have to write the story so that you focus on the uniqueness, not on the stereotypical kid."

"That was my plan. What do you think, William?"

"I think it has potential. I hope you can find these kids out there. Most of the kids I know are pretty straight-up Ivy Leaguers, or at least top-tier college bound. You may have to do some real digging for your story," William starts packing up his bag, ready to head to class.

"I already have two leads on the story, and hopefully once I talk to them I will have a better idea of where to find more kids who have a unique story to share."

"I say go for it, and we can decide based on the quality if we'll run it as the cover story. William, which stories were you considering as well?" Mr. Peterson says, standing up, and therefore indicating that the conversation needs to come to an end.

"Well, we have the fact that Volleyball won the state title again, and we also have the story about teen suicide we could run," William says, as he and Mr. Peterson start walking to the door, William to leave for class, and Mr. Peterson to greet his first block students.

"Tough competition, maybe not the Volleyball story, but that suicide story is good. I quickly read and edited it yesterday. Kirsten nailed it. I will have a draft of my story for you by Friday, William. See you in class!"

As she packs up and walks out of class, she is reminded of the cheating issue she discovered the day before. She thinks she wants to do a story after this one on the cheating epidemic going on at Chain Bridge. Maybe she can do some investigative reporting and uncover a cheating ring. This is what she loves the most about being a journalist, all the amazing stories out there, and often unearthing a topic is much more effective in stopping it than simply reporting it to administration. It makes it a topic of conversation and forces people to discuss it and decide where they stand on the topic.

Today's' track practice is much easier, since it is the day before the big meet, and Coach wants to make sure that the runners are rested and ready. Coach has told Addison that she will be running the 800 and the 4 x 800 relay. She is excited because she thinks she can finally get the time she has been aiming for the in the 800. The state record is 2:12:23, and she thinks she can get close. At the last meet she had a 2:14:58, which would put her third in the state. This is the last regular meet of the season, and next week is the conference meet. She wants to peak for her best run at regionals, the following week. If she can break that state record, she knows Columbia will look at her for their track team, in addition to her academics. Maybe that record will mean that a possible B in Trig won't matter as much.

Coach has the mid-distance runners do a twenty-five-minute easy run with stretching afterwards.

"Okay runners, make sure you drink fluids and get lots of rest tonight. Do your homework now, so I don't hear your weak excuses of staying up late studying. You are getting out of practice an hour early, so no excuses." Coach's voice booms over the field. He has one of those deep voices that was born to coach teens. It grabs Addison in the gut and pulls her attention away from her phone and her conversations, if she dares to be distracted by them. His voice demands full focus.

After the short practice, Addison seeks out Mason. She has to be honest with herself. She really wants his interview for her story, but she enjoys having an excuse to talk to him. She isn't the boy-crazy kind of girl, but talking to him yesterday was so easy and comfortable, she craves that feeling again. To be herself, instead of the wound-up, stressed-out self she normally feels like. Mason has this relaxed go-with-the-flow vibe about him that she wants access to.

She sees him inside the track, stretching near the shot-put pit.

"Hey, Mason!"

"Hi, Addison. How was practice? Are you ready for tomorrow's meet against Yorktown?"

"Yep, I think I will be getting closer and closer to that record. I need to shave off two-an-a-half seconds...easy as pie, right?" She can't believe she said that. That is not her normal type-A, no-joking attitude. She supposes it is that relaxing vibe he is sending off to her.

"You have it in the bag, girl."

"So, I was wondering if you would mind me interviewing you for a story I'm writing for the news magazine?"

"Sure, I guess. What is the story about?"

"Actually, it was inspired by our conversation yesterday. I was thinking about how you and I both don't have the typical Chain Bridge career goals. I want to write a story about the unique dreams and goals that some CBHS students have. I would love to find a student who wants to work for the Peace Corps, or enter the church, or become a social worker. Just something that isn't your typical McLean, Virginia, high-achieving, goal-setting student. Not to say that what we want isn't high achieving, it just isn't your typical money-making, power-holding career."

"Sure, I can't promise that I will be interesting or that anyone will want to read what I have to say, but I'm happy to answer your questions."

"Great, well, as all journalists are...I'm on a deadline. Do you think I could ask my questions today?"

"Only if we can grab a bite to eat. I'm starving. I'm craving pizza from Rocco's. Can we do it there?"

"Well, sure. But don't you have to get to work?" Addison recalls that he said he has to go to work after school.

"Nope. I don't work."

This is confusing to Addison. She could swear that he said he worked after school. She brushes it off and assumes she either misunderstood him, or he was talking about before he joined track. Despite a tiny lump of concern in the pit of her stomach, she moves on. "It won't take that long, but I'm hungry too, and I'm sure my mom is making some crazy organic dinner with eggplant tonight."

"Good Lord."

Addison knows her mom won't mind, but she wants to let her know where she is, so she sends her a text: *Don't get too excited, but Mason wants to grab food while we talk about the story. Do you mind?*

Just as expected, her mom responds almost immediately: *OMG! Exciting. Is it a date? Of course you can go.*

Her mom is both cute and annoying. She has termed a phrase for people like her mom: adorkable. She is such a huge excitable dork, that she becomes adorable. Maybe if she had siblings, Addison's mom wouldn't blow every single little detail of her life out of proportion. Sometimes it feels like her mom was meant to have five kids, and is placing all the love, worry, excitement and general mothering on her... five kids worth. It would overwhelm any teenager. No matter how much she loves her.

Addison texts back: *Mom. it's a story. not a date. i'll text you when I leave.*

Addison and Mason walk to their cars separately. Addison is happy that she can drive herself there and meet Mason. She needs the ten-minute drive to collect her thoughts and figure out exactly how she wants to pose her questions.

Addison starts her Golf. Predictably safe, not overly extravagant and with European influences. The Golf defines her child-hood. Slightly exotic, but not terribly, a little speedily aggressive, but extremely safe. Not too big, yet big enough to accommodate her tall frame, but not too snug. She loves her car. She knows that many of her peers have far more impressive and expensive cars, but hers was her sixteenth birthday gift, and it was a huge surprise. Red, shiny and wrapped in a beautiful bow. Each time she starts the engine, it makes its unique rhythmic thump that almost sounds like a bird's heart racing; she loves the way the sound vibrates through her chest when she pulls out and then its lower vibration when she hits the speed limit.

She can see herself driving this car until she is forty.

She leaves the lot, turns onto Chain Bridge Road, which takes her into town. She pulls into Rocco's Pizza at 3:30, ten minutes after she leaves Chain Bridge High. Mason pulls in right before her and climbs out of his gigantic pick-up truck. She smiles to herself and realizes that the car suits Mason perfectly. It is large, robust, but has that easy rhythm to the diesel engine; the grey color causes her to underestimate the size of the truck, like its owner, whose size surprises her when she walks up next to him.

Addison is amazed again when she approaches Mason; he makes her actually feel small. She only feels small next to her dad. Even boys who are taller than she are often not tall enough to make her feel small, they may have an inch or so on her, but it feels like they are the same size. But with Mason, she actually has to look up at him. The top of her head must just reach his chin. She imagines placing her head on his chest... No, she erases that image from her mind. This is a working meal, not a date. He has been gracious enough to meet with her to talk about his plans for her story in the magazine. Not because he wants her to nestle her head on his chest... *Addison, pull yourself together* she thinks to herself.

They walk into the crowded and dimly-lit Rocco's. It is a small family owned business that has been around for as long as anyone can remember. The current owner inherited the restaurant from his mom, and both mother and son live in separate houses a few blocks from the restaurant. There is always a crowd, no matter the time of day. It seems like people in the community always crave pizza or pasta, and the friendly intimate ambiance. It almost feels like you are at a close friend's house for dinner. The mixed aroma of pizza, pasta, basil, onions and the sweet contrast of soda wafts through the air. Addison is unusually hungry. When she realizes that it is only 3:30, she wonders if the excitement of this story has made her hungry.

Mason and Addison slide into a booth and she pulls out her notebook and flips to the page with the questions she jotted down in class.

"You were serious, weren't you? I was kinda hoping it was a trick to hang out!"

"Dead serious."

Mason looks at her as she pulls her caramel hair into a hasty bun and she grins at Mason. Her green eyes twinkle and her small dimples appear. When she smiles, her white teeth show; they are borderline too big for her smile, but somehow combined with her dimples, she is adorable and rather pretty. No one would say she is a beauty, but she has an appeal that makes everyone around her want to talk to her and be part of her life, even if just for a moment.

The waitress comes to their table to take their order.

"I think we need a minute to decide what we're ordering," says Mason.

"No problem. I'll be right back."

Addison thinks about her research from last night. She wonders where this waitress has come from. She has a slight accent. Could she be commuting to work here, or has she moved here to hold a job as a waitress?

"So, pizza or pasta, girl?" Mason has a bit of a Southern drawl to his speech. Addison doesn't notice it in each word, but she can hear the country roots in his phrases — "girl" comes out sounding like he's from the deep South, rather than Northern Virginia, with a lot of extra lllls at the end.

"Well, I wouldn't mind a few pieces of pizza as long as it isn't too greasy, but I want to order a salad too. Have to balance those carbs and grease with some greens, as my mother always says." Now she feels like a dork. Who brings their mom into either a) a business interview, or b) a date? Either way, she's blown her credibility. Note to self: don't bring mom into the discussion when meeting with a cute boy.

"Any type of pizza you're craving?" Mason's dark brown eyes bore into her. Is he always this intense?

"I'm a veggie lover, I like anything in that category, except onions. But I'm happy to have some meat too. You?"

"Well, considering I'm a farmer... just kidding. I do like my veggies as much as the next guy, but I love my meat too. What if we get a veggie pizza, without onions, with some sausage on it too? Sound good?"

"Perfect."

The waitress returns and takes their orders, pizza a side salad for Addison and two waters. No soda or sweets the day before a big meet.

Now that they have the ordering down, it is time to open her notebook and ask her questions. Then they can enjoy their meal once it gets to the table.

"Do you mind if I record this on my phone? I want to be able to go back and make sure I have the facts right. Sometimes taking notes takes the context and tone out. I'll take notes too, but I still want a recorded version."

"Sure. I don't mind at all. You can listen to it as often as you like." Mason winks at her. Was he flirting with her? Addison reminds herself once again that she is here to write an important story. Mason is a source.

"Okay. So, Mason, has farming always been a dream of yours?" Simple question first. Addison always remember that a journalist wants to make the interviewee feel comfortable with the conversation so they relax. So she asks the easy questions first.

"I think so, I grew up on the farm when I was little, and weekends on the farm were my favorite. I always have loved the smell of the earth and watching the plants grow. Waking up to the misty mountains, well, it's such a contrast to waking up to traffic rolling down Dolly Madison Parkway. Here, it takes twenty minutes to go one mile in rush hour. There, if I take my truck out and drive twenty minutes, I've traveled through my own land; everything I see, we own. It's pretty wicked."

"Do you think your parents want you to become a farmer?" A more difficult question. Addison believes that no matter where someone grows up, or who their parents are, there is always the struggle between what the teenager wants and what the parents want. It is a natural drive for teens to want to make their own way, and it is a natural urge for parents to want to impart their experience and knowledge to lead those same teenagers. A situation ripe for tension.

"No, I don't think so. I think my parents wanted to give me the opportunity to break away from a life on the land. That's why they wanted me to attend Chain Bridge High. They wanted me to have the opportunities of a suburban kid, to be able to become a lawyer, an entrepreneur or a doctor. They didn't want me to be saddled down by the land, having to spend weekends farming. It actually makes me sad because I feel like they undervalue their own work and contribution. My dad has been successful. He runs the farm like a business. He found a niche that is unique and original, he bought land when it was cheap, and he employs people who are loyal to him. He is smart about equipment, he repairs it when it's worth it, he understands mechanics, and he knows when it is time to retire a tractor or a combine. My dad couldn't do his job without my mom. She supports him, she markets our produce, and she's really good at it; I mean, she could be marketing for a huge business in the city. She gets the target purchasers, appeals to them and knows how to make them feel like they are her only client. She is one of the most resourceful women I know. She's even started her own line of organic beauty products and soaps that are making their way into the 'McLean Market' ... I'm sorry. That was a rant. It makes me mad that they don't see how smart they really are. And the problem is, the rest of the 'McLean World' doesn't value them. It doesn't matter that Dad probably makes more than their daddies do, he's still a redneck."

"I get it, Mason. Some people are narrow minded. It's not a rant. I'm not in the same situation, but my dad is one of "those" dads. Derrick Erhard the Third is a successful investment banker. He took over his own father's investment banking business, Erhard Financial Services. He basically was groomed to be an investment banker, like his daddy. He attended the Boston College and majored in business administration and finance; then got his Master's in finance from The University of Pennsylvania. When he graduated, he walked right into Pop's office and began taking over. It was a beautifully orchestrated takeover. Nothing would have made Daddy happier than his precious little princess following his footsteps. Top five school, business and finance, and I take over the D.C. branch of his business. The only part of that plan that doesn't work out is that I hate money and numbers." Addison sighs and puts her hands around her water glass. The red-plastic chiseled sides are rough from use, having been thrown into the dishwasher a thousand times a week. The ice floats on the surface, with the tiny little divots collecting water, causing them to sink slightly, until they tip and resurface. Sometimes Addison feels as if she is that ice cube, floating along, slowly sinking, until she sputters back to life and fights to the surface. Only the ice cube will slowly melt away and become one with the water. Is that her destiny...will she end up settling, melting into the acceptable and expected life?

"So, what is it that Addison Erhard would rather do, than crunch numbers and make loads of money?" Mason is egging her on. Addison knows it. Somehow the interviewee has turned into the interviewer. What would Mr. Peterson think?

"Well," she pauses, "I want to make a difference. Not in monetary terms, or even in the influential political machine in Washington as a lobbyist, I want to really change people's minds, to change their perspective by revealing, reporting, exposing what is really going on in this country and abroad. If people are moved to change the way they think about things, then perhaps policy will really change, an actual adjustment in what Americans value in life. A journalist has the power to influence the way people see the world. If I can break into people's mindsets...I don't know...it's awe-inspiring to think about it."

"I'm not really sure what you mean. Do you really think an entire generation of Americans is going to start reading your articles and change the way that they see the world?" Mason's tone could still be seen as egging her on, as if he is poking her to answer a question he already knows the answer to. Only she is going to take the bait, because now she is all worked up.

"Yes. If I can write for an influential paper and build a reputation for reliable and authentic news. Reporting that isn't bought by the big conglomerates who rule this world, not by lobbyists, but is from the heart, reporting from the ground. A reporter who isn't afraid to write about the oppression of the Palestinians in Israel, even if it isn't considered popular political opinion. Or the fact that the largest commercial companies in the United States market to children under the age of thirteen, knowing that their begging and whining is what drives most of the purchases in this country. Maybe I could write about the fact that the majority of women on this planet are still earning less than their male counterparts who are doing the same work. There has to be a place in this world for the truth." At this point, Addison is flushed and out of breath. Mason sits across from her, grinning.

"Well, I can certainly see that you are passionate about this.

I'm also sure that you realize that there are many, many journalists who have already tried to change the world, and they have either been trampled over by said conglomerates and lobbyists, or killed on the roadside in Syria or Afghanistan, trying to reveal the evil of those regimes."

"Mason, I cannot go on with my life thinking that the truth is futile. I want to impact change, but on my terms."

The waitress arrives with an enormous platter with their "vegetarian" pizza with sausage and Addison's salad...the irony is not lost on Addison.

"Okay, looking at this meal makes me laugh...there is the little sausage in our pizza, trying to make sure we don't eat too healthy..." She attempts to make a cute smile. Addison needs to turn the conversation first to a light-hearted tone, and then back to Mason, who has leaped past interviewer to interrogator and destroyer of dreams.

"Addison, I understand what you want to accomplish, and honestly, I hope you do. It certainly is an honest and well-intended goal, and I think it's worth every effort. There has to be a first for everything, and maybe you will be the first journalist in a long time to make a real difference in the way people see the world around them. Pizza?" Mason uses the pizza server to pull a huge slice of pizza for Addison. It smells delicious and the cheese stretches white and creamy until he is holding it over his head, and it slowly breaks. He places the pizza on a plate and hands it to her. All this passionate conversation about journalism has made her hungry.

"Okay, Mason...this is supposed to be your interview...You are an expert at diverting attention from yourself. Back to the point — how do you think that other kids at school see your different aspirations for your future?"

"Well, I can tell you that the people who know me obviously aren't surprised, because I follow my heart, and I have always known what I want; sometimes that makes me stubborn and ornery, but ultimately, it makes it clear what I want. But, people in our school who don't really know me, from my counselor, my teachers to my peers are flabbergasted. In this environment kids start in Kumon Math and Reading tutoring when they are three to start mastering math skills so that they will be deemed 'gifted and talented'; they get tutors when they start school, join the correct sports teams and parents orchestrate their class selection, all of this geared towards getting into the best school possible...well I'm an anomaly. I can't think of another student at Chain Bridge High School who wants to be a farmer when he graduates. I can think of many students who want to attend Virginia Tech, but they aren't attending for Agriculture."

"So, how do most people react when they hear what you want to do?"

"You mean after they pick their jaw up off the ground?" Addison thought about her mom's reaction yesterday. But Addison hadn't reacted that way. She thought it made Mason intriguing, unique, and passionate about his future. "At first they ask me to clarify. When I say I want to study agriculture, and that Virginia Tech has one of the best schools in the country for agriculture, they start to deflate a little. Then I explain that my father owns lots of farmland, not just a small farm, but multiple farms he has acquired as people have left to pursue city or suburban careers. I finish with the fact that my father's farm is one of the most successful farms in the state, which I want to continue in my family's long tradition of farming. Some kids give me a blank look. Some kids start to understand when I say that my dad owns a lot of land. Others get it when I explain it's like inheriting any family business, that it's established and makes money. Those whose opinion I value see the importance of people like me to the success of our nation. The others, well frankly, I don't care what they think of me, and I don't think I care about what they are going to do when they finish with this place, either, so it's mutual. They either get it, or they don't."

"So you are saying that your friends get it because they know you, and the others make a connection with their associations with success; those who have preconceived notions of farmers as rednecks don't matter to you?" Addison looks at Mason; she is astonished that he has such confidence in who he is. She supposes that in some ways, her dream to be a journalist is similar; however, in other ways she is like her peers in that she wants to be a success, have an impact and attend the best university possible; she is willing to do anything to make it into that school...sports, clubs,

SATs, you name it, she is prepared to make that sacrifice to buy into the system. To her it is a means to the end.

"Pretty much."

"So, in your opinion, are there other students like yourself, who are choosing unusual careers at Chain Bridge High?"

"I think so. Take Jamison Randall — He's in my AP Bio II class. I don't know him well, but he says he wants to join the Peace Corps between his undergraduate and graduate school. He plans to earn his master's in public health and he is planning on spending two years in Africa helping people get proper nutrition. He talks about it all the time in class. He's a bit of a nerd I think."

"I know Jamison, he's friends with Campbell. That is a pretty unusual career path. I don't think that I know anyone who has spoken to me about giving up two years of their lives to charity. I'll most certainly ask Campbell to get his number for me."

"Are you going to take him to dinner too?"

"No, Mason, this is a special circumstance." Addison drops her eyes down to her plate. She can't believe she is flirting again. She can't help herself. Mason puts her in a mood she isn't accustomed to. She is finding herself opening up more than she ever has before, and she is flirting shamelessly.

"Excellent, I was worried this was your standard mode of operation, and I was kinda enjoying thinking that maybe our interview was special." Mason looks Addison straight in the eye. His words hold humor and a lightness of attitude, but his eyes are incredibly serious. Those deep brown eyes, with a small flicker of gold contrasting with the dark chocolate. They beg her to answer in an equally honest and serious manner.

"No, I've never had this long a conversation with anyone I've interviewed, and I've never shared as much with any interviewees. This has been an altogether unique experience for me." Addison looks directly into Mason's eyes when she answers. She wants him to know that she is equally serious and affected by their connection. Addison realizes that perhaps she is being naïve, that possibly what she is feeling is her first experience with a crush, but she can't help think that she and Mason have an unusual connection. She doesn't believe in love at first sight. She is far too practical for that, but she does believe that you find people who you connect with immediately, people who you feel comfortable with right from the beginning. Her relationship with Campbell was the same from the start. The moment they met in kindergarten, they connected. She remembers feeling like she had always known Campbell. With Mason it is the same. She feels a connection with him that makes her comfortable in his presence. She can share with him what she isn't comfortable sharing with anyone else. Funny, given the fact that she has known him for a total of twenty-four hours.

"Well, Addison, it's been chill hanging out and talking to you. It isn't every day that I find someone who is willing to understand why I want to be a farmer, and who takes the time not only to listen, but to respect it as well. I can't wait to read your article. But I hope that you'll meet me for another dinner before it's done. Not only would I enjoy hearing what other mysteriously rebellious McLean teens you've uncovered, but I'd just like spending some more time with you."

"I would love that, and I may need to pick your brain a little more anyway. Maybe we can do something this weekend. I have to spend the next few days working on this, and my Russian project as well."

Mason polishes off the last piece of the pizza as Addison scrapes the last bit of feta cheese and olives from her Greek salad into her mouth. As she chews she sheepishly looks up at Mason, "Not really lady-like."

He laughs, "And me stuffing my face with the last bits of pizza isn't gentlemanly either. It's really nice to see a girl eat and enjoy food. So many girls our age are so concerned about what they eat, and how they are perceived. It can't be realistic, or healthy. Especially for an athlete. I love it."

"I'm going to guess that I could probably out eat you. I know my parents look at my food intake and can't believe it. My mom says I eat as much as two boys. I'm not sure that's true, but I do love my food. It's a good thing I love running too, I guess."

She sees the waitress approaching their table with the check. Oh, that awkward moment...does she pay for the check because he was being interviewed, would he think she is spoiled and too pushy? She decides that since it was for her story, she will pay, she doesn't want to owe Mason anything.

"I'll take that." She hands her credit card to the waitress and the transaction is done before Mason can even reach for his wallet.

"Well, that was a little bit of a dirty trick. You know that the people of Papua New Guinea have a gift economy. They give gifts to each other to make sure that they're forced to remain in a relationship. If you give a gift to a neighbor, then they owe you a gift, and you know that you will see them again in the future, once they give you a gift in return, usually of greater value, then you owe them again, and you now must see them. So, I'll consent to you paying for my meal in the gift economy belief that this will obligate me to return the favor, plus some. So, I'll take you on an adventure on Saturday, if you are free, *and* treat you to something to eat, even better than pizza."

"I think the Papua New Guineans are onto something. How on earth do you know this?"

"Discovery Channel is amazing."

"One redeemable quality of television, I guess. I hate television. But maybe I'll give Discovery a chance, if they promote a gift economy."

"If they truly believed in that, they would gift us something for watching their shows, instead of charging us!"

"Okay, so Saturday we will go on an adventure?" Addison signs her credit card slip, giving the waitress twenty percent tip, her mom was once a waitress and has impressed upon her the importance of a good tip.

"Yup, but the condition is that the adventure is of my choosing, and you don't get to know what it is until we get there."

"Well, I'm curious now. It'll be fun." Addison gathers up her notebook, her phone and her bag, and stands up. Time to get some homework done.

Mason holds the door open for Addison on their way out, and walks her to her car.

"See you at the meet tomorrow; have fun writing that story tonight."

"Lots more research to do, tonight is dedicated to Russian. 'Discover the various authentic Russian foods served in the nineteenth century' sounds like fun right?" Addison sighs...she hates Russian, but she knows if she wants to report from the Eastern side of Europe, Russian is a huge asset. If they taught Arabic, she would take that. Arabic is her college goal.

"I have to work on my research paper, I think I would prefer Russian foods."

Addison senses that they are drawing out this conversation, neither of them really wanting to say goodbye. She actually feels a physical pull to him. The idea of him getting in his car and driving away actually gives her a sick feeling in her gut. This is insane. *Twenty-four hours, Addison. Really?* She thinks to herself. She may be losing her mind.

"See you tomorrow, Mason." Awkwardly she climbs into her car and waves as she starts it, and pulls out of the parking lot. In her rearview mirror she sees him standing next to his truck, looking after her.

5

A Journalist's Work

Tuesday, February 9

When Addison walks in the front door, her mom jumps off the window seat in the front room and greets her the moment she steps into the foyer; in fact, she is so eager that she beats Chandler to the greeting. Addison is almost surprised when her mom and dog don't both try to jump into her arms. Her mom is like a teenage girl, bubbling with curiosity and intrigue. Addison is irritated as soon as she sees her. She knows that she should be pleased that her mom is interested in her life, and not caught up in her own soap opera drama, like so many other moms she knows, but sometimes it gets really annoying, too.

"So, how was dinner?" She can feel the curious energy vibrating through her mom's being. Her eyes are deeply inquisitive, her small forehead wrinkled in concern. Instead of working in her studio and being creative, she has clearly been sitting in the front room of their home, which overlooks the meandering driveway that winds its way through the wooded front yard, waiting for Addison to come home; likely imagining a million versions of how the afternoon has gone. Addison reminds herself to tell her father to come home earlier if for no other reason than to distract her mother.

Unlike many McLean homes, her parents' house has quite a bit of land. Just as her father inherited her grandfather's business, he also inherited the family home when his father retired to Charleston, South Carolina. The home is built in the Georgian Style, which means it looks like a plantation home: wide, white, with two stories, with large French windows overlooking the front yard. Her home is the very picture of Southern hospitality, with soaring, double-decked columned porches that extend across the facade, and wrap around all four sides of the home with honeysuckle vines so sweet that you can taste it in the air. In fact, if it hadn't been so cold outside, most likely her mom would have been sitting on the front porch, swinging, waiting for her to arrive.

"Mom, could you try to be a bit less obvious? I don't want to jinx the dinner with Mason. I really don't want to talk about it, and I really don't have the time either."

Her mother's face brightens, as if she hasn't heard her daughter's criticism. "So, it was a good dinner, a date?"

"Mom. Yes, and no. That's enough. No more questions or assumptions."

Addison goes directly up the horseshoe staircase which runs along either side of the foyer and meets halfway and then swings back around to continue back up to the second and then third levels. It is a grand foyer, and it matches her father's expansive personality, so much more than her mother's humbler attitude and persona. Addison feels slightly guilty for brushing her mother off, she wishes she could be more patient, but she also wishes her mom would give her a little breathing room and would let her come to talk on her own time.

In her bedroom, she looks at the clock. It is now 5:30. She wants to get to bed by 8:30 so she gets enough rest for the big meet. That gives her three hours to work on her Russian project and do some research on the Peace Corps.

She starts by texting Campbell: *Cams. Just had a kind-a-sorta-date.*

Addison opens up her pink laptop and starts preparing her presentation on Russian foods. She also needs to figure out a few math problems, and like Mason, she has a little research to do for her English class. She tries not to feel overwhelmed and gets to work.

Thirty minutes later, Campbell texts back: *excuse me?*

Yep. with mason.

No way! how'd you do that?

Interview... never underestimate a journalist.

You made up a story so you could interview him? brilliant.

I didn't invent it...he inspired it.

And the difference is...

NM I need a favor – Do you have Jamison's cell?

Ummm ya, but you owe me a full scoop at lunch tomorrow. I want all the deets.

Addison texts Jamison: *Hey Jamison, its Addison, Campbell's friend. Would you be able to meet tomorrow to do an interview?*

Within a moment, Jamison texts: *Sure...whats it about?*

A story about kids who want to do interesting things with their lives. i hear you want to go into the peace corps.

Sure, how about the library at 7? I'll be in the bright green vv sweater.

Addison laughs to herself. She can't believe Jamison already knows what he is wearing. She hasn't even figured out what she is wearing to bed!

After finishing her Russian project, which was fairly simple, her five problems, and a little research for her English class, she begins writing the draft for her story. She would like to get at least two more people to interview. It would also be good to add some balance by finding kids who are happily following their parents' plans for them, or those who want to be lawyers, doctors, bankers and politicians because they have a genuine love and passion for the field. She knows that just as she really feels passionately about being a journalist, there must also be students out there who have dreamed of being surgeons, or enacting public policy, or simply love money.

At 8:30 Addison turns off her computer and pads to her bathroom, which is a spacious room off her bedroom. It is her own private bathroom, not that it matters, because she is an only child, and her mother and father have a suite clear across the house. They wouldn't come across here anyway. But, she likes knowing that in the big wide world, this suite of rooms, her cozy bedroom with window seat, and her own bathroom is her safe zone, her place to withdraw and restore herself. She has always been one of those people who actually enjoys solitude and craves it when she's been too social.

When she is done washing her face and brushing her teeth, and has packed her track and school bags, she crawls into her bed. As she is settling into the pillows and under her soft and fluffy down comforter and quilt, she hears her mom gently knock on her door.

"Addison, may I come in?"

"Of course, Mom," she feels guilty for having been rude to her mom earlier, and now she welcomes a chance to make amends before she falls asleep. She and her parents have always been firm believers in going to bed on good terms. She wishes she had been considerate enough to check in on her mom.

"I wanted to apologize for being overly emotional this evening. I was happy for you that you were out doing something social. You are so busy with your school work and track; you don't do much. I know I loved being with my friends when I was your age, and it seems like your generation is too busy you don't get to enjoy life. So, I was excited for you, not trying to be too nosy."

"I appreciate it, Mom, really I do. I know your heart is in the right place. I was not prepared to talk about the dinner yet. It was a nice time, we talked a lot, and I got some great quotes from Mason for my story."

"I'm thrilled to hear that, and I promise I'll wait for you to tell me what you want me to know...okay?"

"Okay...well, we are going on an 'adventure' on Saturday," Addison smiles, and she can feel her dimples, deep and strong. She can't help it, she is so excited to see Mason again, and excited that they are doing something unusual.

"Well, that sounds fun and I look forward to hearing what your adventure is. Good night, my sweet girl. Just know that I love you and I get carried away in that excitement. Would it be ok if I tell your dad when he gets home tonight?" She strokes Addison's caramel hair and smooths her forehead, ending by cupping her small pointy chin. Her mother looks deeply into her green eyes and Addison can feel the silent message she is sending: *You are my world, my everything.* This time instead of feeling crushed by her mother's love, she feels enveloped by it, secure and safe. She knows if she comes home on Saturday and the date was horrible, her mother will be here with her unconditional and unrestrained love.

"Of course, Mom. Love you too."

Addison burrows deeper into her covers and thinks about her parents. How different her mother's upbringing was to hers, and how lonely she must be. Her dad hasn't even come home from the office yet and it is nearly nine o'clock. She's thinking of her mom's art, and the darkness that shows itself there, and the loneliness of her subjects. She tells herself she is going to make more effort to spend time with her mom. Maybe tomorrow she'll do her homework in her mom's studio, so they are at least together.

As usual, Addison is scrambling to get to school before seven. Although she had packed her bags, she had forgotten to pack her breakfast and lunch; she knows that to have a successful meet, she needs to eat well and hydrate. So, she arrives to the library a few minutes after seven and sees Jamison, easily identifiable in his bright sweater.

Jamison is busy chatting with a group of friends when she approaches him. His is a diverse social circle, with a mix of boys and girls from all backgrounds. It is clear that he doesn't fit into a particular clique, but rather has a wide assortment of friends. She recognizes people from drama, and DECA, as well as other athletes, and some kids from the robotics team as well. It makes her feel comfortable with Jamison immediately, giving her impression that he won't be judging her clothes, or her athleticism, but may be looking for something more interesting about her.

"Jamison? I'm Addison," she holds out her hand towards him, and he takes it, smiling broadly.

Jamison has an interesting look to him. He has clean features, with a long trim nose, almond-shaped eyes which are so dark, they are almost black, in fact; they remind her of Mason's eyes in their depth. He has a wide mouth, with almost delicately feminine lips. He smiles broadly, and reveals white, beautiful teeth. His hair is thick and dark, with a hint of a wave, his skin is almost as dark as his hair. It is hard for Addison to see his heritage. He could be African American, Arabic, South American or Pakistani, or perhaps he is a mixture of different ethnicities. It makes him look exotic, and he is beautiful. His immaculate attention to his clothing is obvious too. In addition to his bright green Vineyard Vines sweater, he has a collared Vineyard Vines button up, with the same colored checks. His soft Polo chinos are ironed perfectly with a crease down the middle and allow little green dragons to peek out above his pristine desert boots. With expertly groomed black hair, he's more immaculately put together than Lady Gaga ... no girl can compete.

"Hiya, how's it going? I've heard so much about you from Cams. You're lucky to have such a devoted friend," Jamison takes her hand in his, warm and soft, clasping hers with both his hands.

"I truly am. I love her. So, she was telling me a little about you, she says that you're interested in going to the Peace Corps eventually?"

"Yes, I wanna study international health, and I'd love to work abroad someday, treating the malnourished in third-world countries."

"So... I'm writing an article for the school magazine about students who are pursuing atypical studies and career paths. Could I interview you for the article?"

"Cool, that sounds like an awesome story, gives some of us black sheep a little bit of publicity. I like it. I know a few more of us who want interesting careers...Monique Amad is into theater and wants to study in New York City. She'd be an amazing person to interview."

"Wonderful. Is now an okay time to ask some questions?"

"Yep, I have to make sure I'm on time to class, I already have two tardies; one more and I'll have detention, and I don't have time for that."

"Okay, I'll jump straight in, why'd you choose the Peace Corps?"

"Well, there are two pieces to that story. First, I'm passionate about helping the malnourished in third world countries. My mom is a doctor, but I don't want to work on the fixing of problems, but help these people eat well so that I can prevent illness, which is why nutrition interests me more than being a doctor. Secondly, I would like to bring awareness of the malnutrition in the third world. Working first-hand as a volunteer before graduate school will give me that experience before I learn about policies and strategies."

"Wow, I didn't realize kids in high school were looking that far ahead; do you think your foresight is unusual?"

"Not really, I mean, maybe in the sense that I've done my own research, but I think most kids at Chain Bridge High have a ten-year plan, don't you?"

"I suppose so. What about your mom? She's a doctor, right? How does she feel about you pursuing a career in nutrition instead of becoming a doctor?"

"She thinks it's a mistake. She believes that I can achieve more by being a physician, because I could help both prevent and heal diseases. But I think if I study medicine I'll be pulled into the machine and focus on the healing piece instead of prevention. I'd like to spend most of my life abroad working with the communities you read about in *National Geographic*. I don't want to spend my life 'healing' kids with ear aches and gluten intolerance," Jamison leans back in his chair and defensively crosses his arms over his chest. His body language is telling Addison as much about his feelings as his words do. It tells her he is used to having this discussion and having to defend his point of view and his plans. She imagines many late night conversations between his parents and him.

"What does your dad think?" Addison watches him carefully to see how he will react.

"Well, my dad is a lobbyist. He thinks the answer to everything is to go to law school and then work at changing laws. He says I should help fight for the Red Cross lobby if I want to make a change in world nutrition. I disagree. For me, making a change means being part of the ground forces in the battle."

"Interesting, so where are you applying to college?"

"For undergraduate, Florida State, even though it's the second best choice for nutrition, but I love Florida, and they have a great exchange program, too. Otherwise, Michigan State has a great program; that is the runner-up."

"When does the Peace Corps play into your plan?"

"I'll apply during my senior year of college, and I'd like to go as soon as I graduate. It'd involve spending two years working in nutrition with a third-world population, and then I'd come back to the states for my Masters in International Health. There are several universities which work with the Peace Corps in offering a masters after the two years."

"Okay, last question: How do other kids react to your plans?"

There go his defensive arms again. "Well, my closest friends like Campbell, obviously know me, and most of them are bucking the Chain Bridge High system too, so that isn't a problem, but there are lots of kids who think I'm insane for wanting to volunteer two years of my life, and that I'm willing to travel to a third-world country and live with the native population. As educated as our student body is, people can be ignorant. They worry about AIDS exposure and diseases that the people might carry. They don't understand that we have some of the best doctors traveling with us, but also, many of these diseases are diseases we've been immunized for and our first-world health and strong immune systems protect us from the majority of the diseases we are exposed to. So, I think the risk is low, and the benefits far outweigh any risks that I might be exposed to; in other words, I don't care."

As he finishes, the warning bells clangs through the otherwise quiet library.

"Jamison, thank you so much for doing this interview. These are great answers and they'll add a lot to my story. Do you think that Monique will answer some of my questions too?"

"I'm sure she will, I'll drag her here with me in the morning. Same time, same place. Have a fabulous day, Addison!!"

"Thanks, Jamison! See you tomorrow."

They each go their separate ways, and Addison settles into her math class. It's survival; she reminds herself again.

6

Meeting at the Track

Wednesday, February 10

Addison makes it through the rest of her Wednesday classes, and about a half hour before the end of the school day, track athletes are released to board the bus and head to Yorktown High School in Arlington to compete in their last regular meet of the season. Addison is worried. She has been hydrating and fueling her body all day, and she got enough sleep, but her body doesn't feel tense and ready to spring along the track, and drop less than a second to reach her goal of a 2:12:23. She is currently ranked third in the state, but she wants that record. Only two more meets to make that goal.

As Addison climbs up the bus steps, her stomach is tight. She can feel it rise to her throat, tightening and then dropping right back down until it feels like it has dropped right out of her. This sensation has been happening since lunch, in waves, when she started to visualize her races. She is so nervous, she feels sick. She knows she can't let her nerves sap her strength and energy. She needs a good six minutes of total concentration and all-out speed today. Right now she can't even imagine how she will make it to the start.

She finds an empty seat halfway down the bus. She doesn't want to talk to anyone. She needs to visualize and listen to her music and pump herself up. Maybe she needs to add meditation to her routine to help calm her nerves. There is a fine line between having just enough anxiety and adrenaline to push her past the finish line at her fastest speed, and having so much anxiety that it consumes all her reserves, leaving her feeling sluggish and empty at the start of her race.

The 800 meter is long enough that there is some time and distance to make up for a split second delay on the start, but short enough that runners can't have an easy start and fast finish, as opposed to running the mile or two miles. In some ways, she wishes Coach had put her into the mile instead of the 800 relay. Even though it is longer, it has a completely different feel and pace to it than the 800. The 800 is almost a full sprint, but not quite. She does have to pace herself for the first 200, but then she has to kick it in and speed up every 100 after that. By the last 100 she has to be full speed. Because the 800 is such a difficult distance for most runners, it has become her specialty.

If she were running the mile, however, she would have time to get started, find a comfortable place in the pack to reserve energy, strategically placing herself towards the outside as the race progresses, so that during the last 100 she can swerve to the out and sprint past her opponents. If she kicks it in too early, then she risks a response from another runner, but if she can manage to sprint away without someone tagging along behind her, she can usually maintain a sprinting speed that others can't hang onto.

As she is contemplating her races, she puts her headphones on, and she listens to the songs that keep her going…The Wombats, "Wildcat! Wildcat!" "Back to Back," "Childish Gambino" and "Step Put" by Jose Gonzales. As she pulls her long body into a Z shape, with her knees at eye level with her face, pressed up against the seat ahead of her, and her feet dangling, almost reaching the floor, she settles in. Her eyes are closed and she is trying to block out the bus, the noise and the chatter. Kids are still loading the bus when Addison feels, rather than sees, a large figure standing next to her seat. She looks up to see Mason looking down at her, big brown eyes twinkling and his grin, large as a quarter moon. It actually reminds her a little of the creepy Cheshire Cat in *Alice in Wonderland*, teeth gleaming white under his sparkling eyes.

"Hey, Addison, mind if I sit with you? Most of the seats are taken," he looks sheepish now, because they both know there are plenty of seats, and clearly he wants to share a seat.

"If you think two giants can fit in a bus seat, you are welcome to...but I'll warn you that I'm a bundle of nerves, no fun to hang out with, and may be sick on you. But feel free," Addison is only being half facetious. She is still nervous. But, unexpectedly, Mason is actually a welcome sight. She isn't pulling away from his request like she would have for anyone else, even Cams. She's normally a complete introvert at track meets and wants to be left alone. But Mason has this crazy ability to make Addison comfortable. Perhaps what she needs is a little dose of Mason to calm her nerves.

"I take that as a challenge, since clearly any normal person would take that as a request to mosey on. I'll do the opposite and prove that we can fit in this seat together, and that you, in fact, will not barf in my lap." Mason promptly folds himself into the seat next to her, and tries to sit with his legs neatly placed before him, but Mason is six foot six. He is long limbed and his legs literally cannot fit into the space between the seat and the seat in front of them. He has to mimic Addison and pull his knees up so far that they are almost higher than the back of the seat they are leaning against. As he is maneuvering his body into place, Addison sees and feels how muscular he is. His quads are so big that his uniform track pants are straining at the seams. His feet, dangling just below the bottom of the seat in front of him, are like small planets. They are almost as big as the space allotted for others entire legs. While he is lean, he is not slim. His hip is pressing against Addison's and he angles his shoulders to face her in an attempt to leave her with some personal space.

His arms, which he is attempting to keep on his side of the seat, are enormous. His biceps are solid; and equal to her quads; with forearms like Popeye and the strong hands of Paul Bunyan, Addison blurts out without consideration, "Is there any part of you which isn't huge?"

"Well, my ears are unusually tiny, really. It bothers my mom," he is trying to stay serious, but he can't keep the corners of his mouth from turning up slightly, and the tension of the effort is obvious.

Addison considers his ears. They are rather small, neatly tucked away along the side of his head. He wears his hair closely cropped, but until he mentions it, she hadn't noticed, but now that she really looks, they are almost ridiculously small.

"Seriously, I can't find earmuffs to fit my ears. It's a huge problem for a farmer." Now his attempt at seriousness evaporates, and his restrained smile breaks loose, revealing those beautiful teeth again.

"Okay, Mason, I don't think I'll ever see you in the same way again. All I can see are those tiny little ears placed on that melon of a head. Can you even hear anything?"

"Nope, nearly completely deaf. That's why I like farming, the animals don't require me to hear them."

Now they are both giggling and Addison can feel herself relaxing and unwinding. She really needed to laugh and decompress.

"Well, if you must know, I have a tiny head. It's the only petite thing on me. Where my 6'0" puts me at the ninety-eighth percentile, my head has always been in the thirtieth percentile. My pediatrician was actually worried that there was a problem with my skull." She is trying to be serious again, trying to control the giggles that are fighting to escape from her lungs.

"Well, that certainly explains an enormous amount about you, doesn't it?"

Addison punches him in his shoulder, "Ouch!"

"Serves you right...evidence of that small little head, what did you expect would happen when you punch a farmer? We aren't made of marshmallows you know."

"I'm not mentally challenged because of my small head, Mason! I will have you know that the Romans and Greeks both had small heads. I have been told that I have the build of a Roman statue. It's a sign of nobility. Unlike yours, which is the size of a melon...isn't that what Neanderthals had?"

"Ouch. Touché. Okay, so once I read your article, I will decide if you have the brains of a Roman philosopher or of a Roman slave."

They relax as the bus starts up and rambles out of the parking lot. Yorktown High School is only a twenty-minute ride away, so they don't have to be squished into this position for long, but Addison doesn't mind; Mason's size and attitude make her feel relaxed and calm. Much calmer than she had been when he first sat down next to her.

When the bus pulls into the Yorktown High School parking lot, Addison feels the small tremors of tension in her belly again. She decides this is okay because she knows some tension will actually benefit her in the race.

Her first event is the 800 individual event. This is good for her, because she wants to have the most energy for this event. She needs to start peeling seconds off her time today. If she can drop half a second and come in at 2:14:00 she will be pleased. She basically needs to shave off half a second every meet between now and states, and she can make the record. It's a long shot, but she really, really wants this.

Addison and Mason step off the bus and make their way to the team area. They unload their bags and pull off their warm-ups so they can get ready in earnest for their events. Addison wants to find Coach Turner to talk about her event. Mason heads towards the shot-put pit for his warm-up.

Addison sees Coach Turner. As usual, he is surrounded by his runners, all excited and nervous. She wants to have a chance to talk to him, but she knows the sprinters are the priority since they run first. He gives directions to the sprinters, and finally Addison catches his eye.

"Hey, Addison, you ready for today? Got your race head on?"

"Yeah, I think so. My goal today is to take off a half second. Think I can do that?"

Coach looks at Addison with concern in his eyes. "If you can keep you head in the run, if you can put hundred percent in there, and make no mistakes — that means you are off the block the instant the gun goes off, it means you stay near the front during the race, and that you kick it in hard for the last 300, and as you come around that final bend, put in 110 percent. If you can do that, I think it's in your ability to take that kind of time off."

Addison needed to hear that. She needs to know that Coach knows that she can do this, that her goal is realistic. "Okay Coach, I'm on it. What kind of warm-up should I do?"

"I want you to run *very* slowly for fifteen minutes. Then do some dynamic stretching...kicks, lungs, some squats, and then run another two laps *slowly*. Then sit, stretch a little more, and I want you to visualize your race. From the start to the finish. Move by move. Got it?"

"Got it. Thanks, Coach," Addison turns and starts to walk towards the track.

"Addison!"

"Yeah?"

"I know you have this in you, kiddo. Make it happen."

"Okay, Coach."

Addison walks to her track bag, has some water and puts in her earbuds. She puts on her favorite 80's playlist, channeling the greatest hair bands of all times, and blasts Bon Jovi's "Livin' on a Prayer" — she'll need all the prayers she can get. She starts out running along the outside of the track, doing a slow and steady pace, and she can feel the remnant of Mason's quads along hers, she feels his strong arm along hers, and she realizes that his touch makes her feel warm and strong. She pulls that feeling back into herself, and she feels light and relaxes. She is excited for this meet. She is focused on the goal.

After her warm-up, she sits in the stands and pulls out her bright pink and yellow New Balance spikes. Addison is a size twelve and has always had to special order girls' shoes. She is so used to having to wear and run in men's shoes that when she was able to find women's spikes in her size, she wanted them to be as girly as possible. The shoes make her feel lighter, faster and stronger.

She pulls her spikes on, and strangely she hates running in socks, so unlike many of her fellow athletes, she slides her bare feet into the spikes and tightens them. She stretches and curls her toes, and makes sure that there is a good balance between tight enough to keep her shoes snuggly on her feet and loose enough to allow her toes to move and settle into the toe box.

After all the shorter sprint events, the announcer calls out the warning for her event, the 800. She places her phone, headphones and warm-ups into her bag and walks onto the track to get ready for her event. She is nervous, but she is the kind of nervous that actually makes her muscles tense and responsive. She knows that her body is fully fueled and her muscles are itching to start and run fast.

Addison waits for her heat. She is in the last and fastest heat. Because her recorded time is the fastest, she is placed in the middle of the heat, along with three other runners, in the center position. This puts her at a natural advantage, because unlike those in the outer lanes, she doesn't have to maneuver into the middle of the pack. She is automatically placed in the center and that makes her run more efficiently.

She places her feet hip width apart, with her right leg forward, and bends down into a running position, with her arms bent, as if caught in mid-stride. Her entire body is tense and ready to release energy when the gun goes off. She waits to hear the gun's report resonate through her body, marking the start of her race.

The official says, "On your mark, get set..." Boom! The gun shoots its blank. Addison's body starts with minute movements forward with "on your mark," so that when the gun goes off, she is already moving forward. This was a great start, almost too good. She is in the lead, which is less than ideal; she would rather have someone else breaking the wind for her, but going into this meet against Yorktown, she already knew that she would likely be the fastest runner and lead the way. She has a lead of about two leg-lengths. She is feeling fast, her legs are moving, as if they are running on their own, she can feel the length of each stride, and how far back her kick goes, propelling her opposite leg far in front of her. She knows she can't go too fast, too quickly.

After the initial 100 meters, Addison tries to settle into a rhythm so that her heart can regain a normal beat. She is still in the lead and making long, equal strides as she runs. She can feel a runner right behind her in her slipstream. Addison has to lose this runner or she will rest in Addison's slip stream, maintaining her energy, only to pass her in the last 100 meters. She sprints a little faster until she knows that her shadow is gone. She tries to maintain this pace, aware that in order to take time off she needs to continue to increase her speed every 100 meters.

As she rounds the last turn of the 800, she kicks her legs as fast and hard as she can, she imagines that her feet are touching her bottom, and she reaches her legs far in front of her, continuing to make each length of her stride longer, but turning over her cadence as quickly as she can. As she nears the finish line, her lungs are burning, her legs have become numb and are rotating on automatic pilot. She pushes as much as she can, even though she has no competition, she wants to shave as much time off her personal best as she can. She crosses the finish line twenty-five meters before second place. She finishes with strong strides and then slows her body down, which almost feels like a plane landing on the runway, trying to slow down unnaturally, putting on brakes and wind resistance as she stands up, trying not to trip or fall.

She stands in the finish area, hands on her knees, trying desperately to catch her breath, the second-placed runner; Samantha Percie pants next to her, "Great run, Addison."

"Nice job, Sam."

"Addison! That was an incredible run!" Mason runs to her as she straightens up and stretches her legs and back.

"Thank you...did you see my time?" She is still panting, trying to catch her breath.

As she asks this, Coach walks up. "That was incredible, Addison! You took off three tenths of a second. 2:13:15. Well done. Make sure you cool down; you have the relay in less than thirty minutes."

"Awesome, Coach. I'll go cool down now."

"Want some company?" asks Mason.

"Sure. I'd love it actually."

Mason and Addison slowly jog along the inside of the track, where they can see all the other events taking place, such as long jump, pole vaulting and high jump. As they pass the shot-put pit, Addison looks to her left at Mason, "Have you gone yet?"

"I've had my first qualifying event. I got a forty-two, so I am pretty happy with that. Hoping to eek out a forty-two and a half for the final." Mason looks non-plussed, as if it doesn't matter to him if he makes his goal or not. Addison knows that forty-two feet is an excellent distance for shot-put, but Mason doesn't seem to truly care. It is so foreign and confusing to Addison.

"So, when is the final?"

"In about ten minutes. Wanna come cheer me on? It might be that little extra I need for that half a foot," he winks at Addison and grins in a way that she already recognizes as being just for her.

"Sure, let's run one more lap and then head over."

After the cool down, which is actually a perfect warm-up for Mason, they head to the shot-put pit. Mason leaves her and goes to practice. He does squats, and he practices his spins. He does his first drill without the shot-put, and then holding the twelve-pound ball next to his neck, at the base of his skull. His shot-put coach is nearby, observing. He spins but does not release the shot-put.

When it is his turn, Mason steps into the circle that contains the shot-put pit, which is filled with hard packed dirt, similar to a baseball field. Reaching out from the pit is a pie-shaped field, marked with white paint, two lines running semi-parallel to one another, only as they go longer, the distance between them grows, the pie is then divided with more lines, running perpendicular, following the curve the of the pit's outer line, each a foot apart, running from one bordering line to the other. So, it looks like a giant piece of pie, divided into sections along the width. The goal is to throw the shot-put as far down the pie as possible. It doesn't matter if it lands to the left or the right, that it is as far as possible.

Mason squats in the pit, with his legs spread far apart. He places the shot-put right up against his neck, as he did during practice, he starts to rotate slowly back and forth, almost like he is winding himself up; and after doing this twice, he unwinds his body, spinning completely around and then again another 180 degrees when he releases the shot-put, hurling it out into the pie. It lands well past the forty-two mark.

As soon as he sees his distance, Addison sees him scan the crowd, until his eyes find hers. He smiles broadly and gives her the thumbs up. Nothing more, no cheer, no fist pump. Just his relaxed private thumbs-up for her.

Mason grabs his warm-ups and walks towards Addison, "You ready to head to your final?"

"That was great, Mason, you threw it exactly where you wanted it; aren't you excited?"

"Sure, as long as it's good enough for VT to take me seriously, I'm satisfied. Felt pretty good though, if I'm gonna be honest. Let's get you to your start; it'd suck if you missed it."

They head across the field to the start area. Mason offers to hold her warm-ups while she runs. This event is the relay, which means she is running one of four legs of the event. She is finishing the relay, because she is the fastest at the 800; it is her job to close the deal, finishing strong. They are expected to win this relay based on the established times for the runners. Addison is happy that this event comes after her individual event, and she has the confidence to know she can run fast, but she also knows that she will feel more fatigued, so she really wishes that she weren't running anchor.

She and her teammates are pretty close. There is Samantha, who placed second in the individual event and who is starting the relay out; then there is Marissa who normally plays leapfrog with Samantha in that their times are similar. There is Tara, with whom she doesn't get along; they never liked each other and they have a bit of a negative competitive relationship. It differs from her rivalry with Samantha. Samantha pushes her to do better; they have a history of beating one another week to week, and they cheer each other on and congratulate the winner. It's fun, and Addison knows that Samantha wouldn't talk behind her back or resent her for breaking the record. Tara, on the other hand, envies her wins, feels that she deserves to win, rather than Addison. Tara has a chip on her shoulder, and for the life of her, Addison can't figure out why. She is concerned about Tara passing the baton to her. She knows that if it was Samantha it would go well, but she worries about Tara. She honestly wouldn't put it past her to make a bad pass and make it look like Addison's fault, so she can make the argument that she should be anchor instead of Addison at the next meet.

She lines up with Samantha, Marissa and Tara. Samantha gets into the starting position, and is off with the gun. She has a strong start, but there is evidence of fatigue from the earlier race in her stride. She is a little sluggish, and she is looking for a comfortable pace. She settles in third place, getting in a rhythm. Addie would have preferred for her to be in second, but third is still good. As long as there is enough room for a clean hand-off and there isn't too much real distance to cover, she thinks they can make up the difference in the following legs.

Marissa gets ready in the hand-off area, slowly starting to move forward as she sees Samantha come along the bend and hit the last fifty meters. Their hand-off is nearly perfect, and Marissa races off, quickly slipping into second place, she maintains her position for the first lap, but then is overtaken by the third-place runner. Addison can see the tension in her legs as she works to maintain her position. The fourth-place runner is about ten meters behind her, but is gaining slowly. As Marissa hits the second-to-last turn, she speeds up slightly, gaining again on the second place runner from Yorktown. She pulls a classic Marissa sprint, and as she comes around the final bend, her legs move more quickly, her arms pump, and she passes the second place runner, and now is gaining on Yorktown's A-team. If Tara can hand off smoothly and quickly, then Chain Bridge's team will win the relay.

As Marissa comes into the exchange area, Tara keeps her eyes on the baton and starts to move slowly forward, with her hand behind her, ready to take the baton. Marissa slows down slightly so that she can place the baton in Tara's outstretched arm. As she reaches Tara, she trips, a little misstep, but it is enough to put Tara's hand just out of reach. Tara sees the misstep, and moves to her right to meet the baton, but this misstep and rearrangement eat enough time for the Yorktown's A-team to increase their lead. Tara is going to have to run the race of her life if they are going to make up the lost time.

Tara sprints out of the exchange, racing and working to make up the time difference. Yorktown has placed their second-best runner in this leg, instead of the first. Samantha would have been a better match, but Tara is putting her all into the run. She slowly eats away at the lead and as she comes through the final bend, Addison gets into position to take the baton. Tara is glaring at Addison, as if to say that she better not waste the time she has made up. Addison's stomach is tight, she is nervous and edgy. She hates the pressure of holding the success of the relay on her shoulders. She looks behind her at Tara's hand, ready to take the baton. Yorktown's A-team is in the exchange with a ten-meter lead. They have a textbook exchange, and their runner is off to a fast start. Addison takes the baton from Tara and heads out of the exchange. She moves to the inside lane. She can see Yorktown's cleats in front of her, a quick rhythm of the runner's quick cadence. Addison is much taller than their runner, and her stride is longer, so she reminds herself to use her own rhythm, instead of matching that of the girl ahead of her. Her lungs are bursting; she can feel the tightness in her hamstrings from the sprint in the 800 individual. She doesn't have as much energy as she had earlier in the meet.

She moves her legs, she pumps her arms, but she can't make up any time on the Yorktown runner. As she comes around the final bend, she is still ten meters behind Yorktown. She doesn't have any more gas in the tank. She can't close the gap. Addison finishes right behind Yorktown. She feels her stomach sink, she knows that her teammates are disappointed in her lack of sprinting, and her inability to make up the difference. As she had worried, Tara is waiting for her, with a scowl on her face.

"I had it all set up for you, Addison; all you had to do is close the gap. Why couldn't you do that? I told Coach he should have put me on anchor. You're too obsessed with your record, and you used up all your speed in the individual event."

"Tara...honestly...I gave it...all I had," Addison is panting, gasping for air and trying to defend her run. She really doesn't like Tara at this moment. She knows intellectually that it was Coach's call, not her own. But she also knows that what Tara says is true. She gave everything she had towards getting her record, she didn't save enough for the relay.

"Well, I'm going to talk to Coach. This is ridiculous," Tara turns on her heel and walks away.

Samantha and Marissa are standing next to Addison, their arms protectively draped over her shoulders, as she continues to try to catch her breath.

"We're sorry we let you down, it's our fault as much as anyone's. None of us were feeling it."

"And I tripped; if Tara should be angry at anyone, it should be me. She wants anchor and the glory. She is setting it up for Conferences next week," says Marissa charitably.

"Thanks, girls. It's all good. She can have anchor, it's too much stress," as she says this, she knows that it's only partially true. Yes, it's a lot of pressure, but she is also proud every time she is placed as the anchor; she gets to take it home, get the glory, and feel crossing the finish line first, even though all four girls work together to get there.

As she stands up she sees that Mason is standing on the sideline, waiting for an opportunity to talk with her. She walks towards him. He is smiling, despite the fact that she lost the race. "Hey, girl!" there is that Southern drawl again. She really likes the way it sounds; it sounds personal, an affectionate term only for her, rather than the generic word that it really is.

"Hey...that didn't go as I had imagined," she is disappointed, and it is evident in her voice.

"I thought it was a solid run. You didn't lose ground, you maintained. Don't forget that you ran only a half hour after your fastest 800. You can't get two amazing races in one day. You got one amazing race and one solid one," his kind eyes bore into her own. They demand that she listen to him.

"I suppose you're right. Tara was pretty angry at me, though — said she had it set up perfectly for me," she looks up into his face, and she sees the gentleness that calms her. *Doesn't he ever get mad?* She thinks to herself.

"Well, Tara could have taken the lead and given you more to go on, especially knowing that you had already run a great 800. If she didn't have it in her to take the lead, why would she expect you to?"

"Good point," Addison wants to stop thinking about it. "I'm going to cool down. Want to come?"

"Only if you promise to let me buy you a chocolate shake later. You know, chocolate is the ideal recovery food, right?"

"Yeah, I know. I do have some homework to do, but I suppose we can get a quick shake," she looks up at Mason sheepishly. She knows that she shouldn't, that she doesn't have the time. She has Trig homework, she has to work for AP Chemistry, and there is her article she wants to work on. She has to have it ready for William on Friday. She can't resist Mason; she wants to spend time with him, and he calms her. He helps put things into perspective.

"Okay, we will run over to Iberry after the meet, have a quick chocolate milkshake, and I will release you to your endless studies."

"Sounds like a plan."

7
The Making of a Story
Thursday, February 11

Early Thursday morning, Addison wakes up feeling tired and sore. She sleepily opens her eyes and looks at the clock. Thankfully she has woken up with the first alarm and she snuggles back in bed with Chandler for a few moments. He is so warm and cozy, and her pillow so soft. The air in her room is cold, and frost spreads across the windows. Addie anticipates the frozen tile floor in her bathroom and she burrows even deeper in her bed, nose up against Chandler's velvety, fuzzy ears. A dog's ears are the softest, sweetest, and most comforting things on earth.

As she lays there, she feels the anxiousness building up. She is meeting Monique Amad and Jamison for an interview at seven, she also has to print her research notes, and she will have a quiz in chemistry today. The anxiety of all that needs to be done gets the best of her, and her bed is no longer a relaxing hideaway from the world, but a place where she is tortured by her own brain and nervousness. She throws back the covers and jumps down from her giant bed. She loves that it's so tall; it makes her feel small and like a little girl.

Addison hustles through her morning routine, throwing on skinny jeans, with a long brown sweater and boots. The sweater accentuates her thin, strong legs, flowing loosely over her jeans and boots. She adds an infinity scarf in earthy tones to keep warm and cozy. She has mastered the layered look, as each classroom at CBHS has its own temperature, ranging from hot and muggy to frigid. She grabs breakfast and her coffee to go. Miraculously, she gets to the library by 6:45 so she can print her research notes. Just as she pays her five cents per copy (which is ridiculous. Isn't this a wealthy school?), Jamison and Monique walk into the library.

"Hey, Jamison. Hi, Monique. I'm Addison. Nice to meet you."

"Nice to meet you too."

"Do you mind if we sit down and I ask questions about college and your future career?"

"Sure."

Jamison, Addison and Monique find a sitting area in the back of the library where they can talk quietly. The library has been recently overhauled; it is modern, yet comfortable: sofas and chairs are placed in cozy combinations so that the occupants can sit and read independently, yet close enough that before and after school kids can meet to study and talk together. Each little sitting area is surrounded by a book section, so it almost feels like a private family room. At the front of the library is the expected check-out desk, but also two treadmills, and three elliptical trainers. This is to encourage kids to get exercise while they read. It's surprising how many kids get up on the trainers in their school clothes and casually walk while they read. Addison thinks it's brilliant. There are also computer banks located near the front, between the trainers and the stacks of books. These are used by students, but they are also used by the librarians to teach research and filmmaking.

The three of them settle into their chairs, Monique facing Addison, and Jamison sitting next to Monique. It strikes Addison as a little odd that Jamison is staying with Monique. She assumed he would introduce them and leave.

Monique is a small girl, with small limbs and a slight frame, everything about her seems tiny, with the exception of her hair and her mouth. She has dark hair that falls down her back, almost to her bottom, thick and wavy. Her mouth is large, but beautiful, and it's the most noticeable feature in her face. Addison imagines that when she sings or speaks onstage her mouth is stunning, almost in the way that Steven Tyler's is. She is dressed in all black, black

71

riding boots, black jeans, a long, draped sweater that reaches her knees, making her seem even smaller, and her nails are painted black as well. She wears no make-up besides dark black eyeliner, which accent her green eyes, and deep red lipstick. She is striking and intimidating, despite her diminutive size.

"So, Jamison tells me that you want to go into theater after high school?"

"Yeah, my freshman year I actually wanted to attend Walnut School for the Arts, it's a boarding school in Massachusetts. At that point, my parents didn't believe I knew what I wanted to do. But I've proven to them that theater is my passion, and I think they understand that I'm good at it. I've begged them to let me transfer, but they're hesitant."

"Do they believe that you might change your mind?"

"I think my dad knows this is who I am, but my mom still hopes that I will become a lawyer like her. Her parents emigrated from Jordan before I was born, and I think she has this reverence for American Law, and she can't understand why I won't choose a career that is guaranteed to bring me accomplishments and success."

"Is she worried that being in theater won't lead to success?"

"Yes. She believes that only a small number of people become successful in theater, whereas most lawyers have lucrative careers, so the guarantee isn't there."

"How do you measure success?"

"To me, success is happiness, it's following your dream, being true to who you are. If I can perform in a small theater, and have people enjoy my shows, understand my characters, if I can reach the audience and move them to feel, then I'm successful. It doesn't matter to me if I make thousands, or millions, I'm alive when I act, and I can't imagine life without that being my focus."

"And your dad supports you?"

"His mother was an actor in Jordan, actually a notable actor. She married a doctor, my grandfather. I think in some ways my dad supports me because he thinks I will marry well. My mom gets angry because she doesn't want me to be dependent on a man for my security. So, there is the big family argument."

"Where do you want to go to college?"

"The Tisch School of the Arts, of course! I know it's a long shot, but I did attend Governor's School for the Performing Arts last summer, as a rising junior, which is a big deal. I've already had some contact with Tisch, but I'm also looking at Joseph Clayes, which is in California, Carnegie Mellon in Pittsburg, and Bucknell University has an amazing performing arts program as well. But I love New York, and I really, really want to attend Tisch. It has been a dream of mine since I was a little girl." Monique's face lights up as she speaks of New York. Addison can identify with her so much, she feels her entire core wake up with the connection; they share a passion for her city, and it bonds them together.

"I completely understand, Monique. I absolutely adore New York; I want to attend Columbia. Not everyone gets it. A lot of people think New York is dirty, too busy, too many crazy people, but it makes my heart sing!" Addison struggles to contain her excitement, she doesn't want to put Monique off, who seems so cool that Addison can't imagine her to be excited by finding someone who shares a passion for NYC.

"Oh, I knew the two of you would hit it off. I knew it!" Jamison excitedly chimes in, as if he has made a match. "Two girls who both love New York!"

"There is something about the activity and energy level that never ends. Inspiring. People can be crazy, creative, dress like idiots or runway models, it doesn't matter. You find your tribe. In the theater world, Broadway is the place to be, to start, to be noticed, it's all there. Attending Carnegie Mellon gives you a foot in the door in many of the big theaters."

"I hope we both end up as New Yorkers. Have you been there recently? My mom is taking me to visit Columbia over Spring Break in March." Addison looks at her with hope in her eyes; the idea of knowing one soul from Virginia, and someone who has the same passion is exhilarating.

"I was there over the summer. Maybe I will ask my dad to take me up during Spring Break too; we can meet up." Monique seems genuine in this, and Addison hopes it happens.

"Just a few more questions, okay?" Addison knows that it is getting long, but she is getting to the really difficult questions, the ones that will give her story the "meat" that she is looking for.

"Sure."

"How do your friends and others react when you tell them you want to attend a school for theater and become a Broadway actor?"

"Well, my close friends all know it's my passion, and even other students are aware that I have been in every play I can get into since I was little. I have performed with the McLean Community Players, and I have been in plays at Dolley Madison Elementary and Old Dominion Middle School. It isn't a big reveal"

"So, in general the response is positive."

"I think it's more expected than positive. I have heard many teachers and friends of my parents' warning that I won't make it big, that only a small percentage of stage actors become famous, but I don't care. It's all good."

"One last question for the story; would you do anything, even upset your mom to attend a theater school?"

"Yes. Anything."

"Awesome. Thanks so much, Monique. And, honestly, I would love to hang out and share our New York stories sometime."

"Well, a bunch of us are going out for dinner Sunday afternoon, if you want to go...my theater peeps all love New York!"

"I'd love to. Jamison, are you going too?"

"Of course," Jamison has been quietly sitting and listening while the girls talked, so much so that Addison had almost forgotten he was there. But now he was coming to life again, gathering up his bag and his coffee mug. "Campbell is supposed to come too, as if you need more reason to come hang out with *moi*."

"Will you text me the details?"

"Absolutely." His answer is almost drowned out by the bell. Time to head back to Trig again; Addison hates having to start every single day with math. Why can't her first block be journalism so she can write? The article is bubbling inside her, begging to come out. As she was listening to Monique, her story was forming in her mind. She thinks she has a good start now, but maybe getting an interview with a typical Chain Bridge student would help too, to show balance.

Addison enters journalism class fired up. She wants to get her story written and bounce some ideas off her fellow editors. William is already in the room, logging into the computer. Addison dumps her bags on the floor next to him. Even though Mr. Peterson doesn't assign computers to staffers or editors, everyone has a station that they have claimed as their own. They always have to share, especially staff writers. However, editors are usually so busy working on editing and designing magazine pages that they monopolize their computers.

"Hey, William," says Addison, "What's up?"

"Just trying to pull some good stories for this edition. We've got a lot of strong articles. I really wish we could add more pages to the March issue. How is your story coming along?"

"Progressing, slowly but surely. I have already done three strong interviews. I would really like to find one more to balance out the story, someone who wants to pursue his or her own dreams, but has the typical Chain Bridge High expectations."

"So, what do you have so far?" William looks away from his computer and turns his full focus on Addison. Addison believes this is why he is such a good editor: he knows when to pay attention, and he makes everyone feel as if they are the only person who matters at that moment. This is a gift of a natural leader, the ability to make those people who they interact with feel special and valued. She is trying to learn to do that as well, to put away the phone, the stories she is editing, and focus on the speaker.

"I have an interview with Mason Gentry, about his dream to go to Virginia Tech and study agriculture, I have Jamison Randall, who wants to study nutrition for his B.A. and then join the Peace Corps, and I have Monique Amad, who wants to pursue theater at Tisch School for the Arts and act in New York. Each person has a really compelling story to tell and feels passionate about their future careers. The most interesting thing to me is that not one of them measures success by how much money they can make, they all value achievement by doing what they want to do, by what would make them happy. Some are going against parents' wishes, some kids have support of one parent, but not the other. It's so fascinating to hear what each of these kids is struggling with to follow their dreams. Most of their friends seem to support them, but there is bias against them from kids who don't know them."

"Maybe you could do an infographic along the side of the story. You could get a staffer to survey kids at Chain Bridge High - would their parents back them up if they pursued an alternative career? Or we could ask if they would consider a career that wouldn't make them rich, but would make them happy. Something along those lines." William is pensively looking right past Addison, she can tell that he is thinking about the story, and the layout and how it will all tie together.

"You know, there are some other stories in the drive for March that could be tied together. Kirsten is writing a story on suicide, and how to get help. That would be a great complimentary article; we could make a magazine that would focus on the stresses of kids in high school, the pressure, anxiety, drive, sports, the need to be in clubs and hold leadership positions. It could be a conversation starter for the school. Why are we all so stressed out?"

Addison loves this idea. She can visualize what the magazine will look like...show-stopping photographs of students, along with hard-hitting stories that appeal to everyone, and her story as the cover story, how to break away from the mold.

"Heather is writing a story about the boys' basketball team and their loss against T.C. Williams. There's a quote from Tim Brooks, that he was tired during the game because he had been up late reading his AP US History assignment and writing a paper, so he wasn't rested. Heather could go back and get more interviews from the boys on the team about the effect that homework has on their performance on the court."

"Great idea, Addison, let's look in the drive to see if there is a story on clubs that we can run too, maybe tweak a little. Next, we need to think of a cover idea. How can we visually portray this for our readers...I say we do a little cover pitching meeting at the start of class. I'll let Mr. Peterson know."

As the bell rings, students settle in the classroom area of the newsroom. Tables are arranged in a U format, so that the students are sitting about the room, all facing the front of the room where William and Addison are getting ready for a pitching meeting.

During the meeting, William and Addison ask students for their input for the cover. They explain the concept for the magazine...stress, expectation, and future for students at Chain Bridge High. Heather already has people she thinks she can interview, and Andrew, who was working on a story about Key Club, says he'll make edits to the story to add in the pressure to be in a leadership position, and why they feel it, and how much time it will take to be in such a position.

Jessie suggests following up with students who graduated four, eight, and fifteen years ago, and find out if all the stress, anxiety, and over-scheduling did lead to successful careers; and was worth it in retrospect. Several students also volunteer to do surveys to add alongside stories.

The class can't settle on a good cover picture, and they decide to keep their eyes open and keep the cover ideas in their minds as they go through their school day and after-school activities. Once they finish brainstorming, everyone starts to work on their projects, some students leave the room to conduct interviews, while others go to their workstations. The lab is new, with new streamlined Macs flaunting shiny large screens and state-of-the-art InDesign software. A journalist's dream.

Addison settles into her chair, opens up her Google Docs and begins writing her story. She sits in the zone, working, writing, and listening to her music for the remainder of the class, as the words pour out of her fingertips onto the screen. This is where Addison is the most comfortable, the happiest. Writing. Reporting. Creating.

After journalism, as she leaves for APUSH — AP U.S. History — she thinks about who her last interview could be. She decides to listen carefully during classes and lunch, and see if she can overhear anyone who will fit the description, and ask a few questions.

Her lunch block is during APUSH, so after lunch, they settle back into their seats to pick up the rest of the lesson. Mrs. Nelson holds a discussion on the taxation system of the United States. As if on cue, Addison finds the perfect person to interview.

"During the Industrial Revolution it was important that the government reorganize their tax system. Henry George offered up a single taxation rate. What do you think are the benefits or detriments to a one taxation rate?" Mrs. Nelson might as well have dropped a bomb in the middle of class. One thing the children of wealthy parents would hate: if there were to be a single tax rate.

"Why should I support the lazy people who won't work? They should get a job and pay fair taxes. Fair taxes aren't even taxes. It should be an equal burden," Stephanie Burkes emphatically states. She is clearly passionate about this subject of taxes. This might be a person who would be perfect for her story topic. Addison sits back and waits to hear more. She considers playing devil's advocate.

"Well, why wouldn't it be fair to tax everyone the same? That sounds fair to me. Equal parts of the pie." Mrs. Nelson is egging her on.

"Because, if I make three million a year, and I'm taxed fifteen percent, then I'm paying three hundred k in taxes. If someone else makes thirty k a year, then they only have to pay three grand. The guy making three mil is working hard for that money. Why should he pay more than a quarter-mil in taxes, while the teacher, or baker, or mechanic only has to pay four and half-grand? They should work harder, or get a better job." Bingo. Addison has her interview.

Addison raises her hand; she can't resist to play devil's advocate.

"Addison?"

"So, are you saying, and pardon me, Mrs. Nelson, that a teacher isn't working as hard as someone who is a millionaire?"

"Yup, no offense Mrs. Nelson, first, you get your summers off, so you don't even work all year, and then, if you wanted to earn more money, you could find a better paying job. I don't think that because of someone's career choice I should be paying more to support the government. Why would my dad have started his own practice only to pay it to the government? Yes, he makes a lot of money, but he also took the risk, worked the late nights, hired people, and now he even has to provide health insurance for all his employees, which is already costing him an arm and a leg. Why should he pay even more to support those same people he is employing and paying for health care? I'm planning on working with my dad after college, and the idea that all our hard-earned money is going to taxes sucks."

Addison doesn't want to aggravate her more, her goal was to see if she could find out what Stephanie plans on studying, so she can approach her after class and ask for an interview. She lets Stephanie have the last word.

"Okay, class, this has been entertaining, but I want to redirect our discussion to the late nineteenth century America and their taxation situation."

Mrs. Nelson continues the discourse, focusing on the Industrial Revolution, and Addison listens in, but she is also busy formulating questions she can ask when class is over.

After the bell, Addison, already packed up and ready to go, steps out of the classroom, and waits outside the door for Stephanie to come out.

"Hey, Stephanie! I'm a writer for the news magazine and I was wondering if you would be interested in letting me interview you for a story I'm writing for the March edition."

"Um, sure? What's the story about?"

"The article is about careers kids at Chain Bridge are planning on pursuing, and it sounded like you already know exactly what you want to do and even where. You're perfect for my story."

"Oh, okay. Now?"

"No," Addison smiles, "I need at least fifteen minutes for the interview. Do you think you could meet at the library at seven tomorrow morning, or after school today?"

"I don't come in early. Can we meet at Starbucks after school? I can't stand being in these halls a second after the bell rings. Two-thirty, Starbucks right off Chain Bridge Road?"

"Man, I have practice at 2:45. Do you think we could meet in the parking lot instead of Starbucks? Maybe 2:10?"

"Fine, I guess. I'm at spot forty-three. Silver Mercedes."

As soon as the bell rings, Addison quickly rushes to the locker rooms so that she can be changed and be ready for practice when she heads to the interview. She grabs notebook and phone and walks to the parking lot.

When she gets there, Stephanie is waiting on the hood of her car. She is fairly short, without being "short." She has long, shiny blond hair that cascades over her shoulders and down her back. Addison wonders if she is one of those girls whose hair is naturally straight and glossy, or if she spends money and time straightening it. Either way, despite the fact that Addison's first impression of Stephanie is that she doesn't like her well, she can't deny that Stephanie is beautiful, in the "classic American beauty" standard. She is lean and muscular, despite the fact that she doesn't look like an athlete. Her clothing is immaculate, with brown Tory Burch riding boots, dark black Seven of Mankind jeans, and a cashmere sweater snuggly fit along her curves. She is wearing a short flight jacket, showing off her trim figure. Her make-up is chic, making her skin look perfect, yet she has avoided the caked make-up look that many of her peers have. She is striking, and she knows it.

"Hey, Stephanie, thanks for meeting me and working with my schedule."

Stephanie looks at Addison and gives her a plastic smile. "No problem."

"So, I'm really interested in finding out why you decided to pursue law, in your father's footsteps."

"Let's see, my dad owns a really successful practice, so it would be kind of silly not to join him in his practice. I mean, I would be partner on day one, versus working my way up in another industry, and having to wait like ten years to make partner. Besides, my dad went to Yale Law School, and since he's an alum and I have good grades, I should be able to get in no problem." Stephanie's manner isn't curt, but it is dismissive, as if she can't be bothered with real life circumstances. She expects the easy way in.

"How long have you wanted to be a lawyer?"

"Honestly, as long as I can remember. I used to go into my dad's office with him on the weekends. He worked every single weekend, both days. I would play with the computers, and I would write and sign letters to clients. I'd pretend that I was in front of a jury and argue why my cat was innocent in the death of our pet mouse, because it was in her nature. Looking back, it was actually pretty cute. I loved being there; the smell of the papers, it's almost like a library, quiet, lots of paper, people working on their cases. And because I'm the boss's daughter, I was treated well, the secretaries brought me sodas and treats. I have great memories." Suddenly, Addison can feel a change in the tone of Stephanie's attitude. She has gone from sounding entitled, to truly having a connection with the firm, and an understanding of the job and why she wants to be there.

"So, what kind of law does your father practice, and will you practice the same?"

"He practices corporate law. He writes contracts, settles disputes, advises clients on what they can and cannot do legally, and when they make a mistake, he tries to help them out of it. It's actually pretty cool, because he has some big clients, and he talks about them to me when I hang out in his office. All client-confidentiality, so I can't share that with you, but it is pretty incredible to be on the inside of the case, to know what's really going on."

Addison laughs, "I'll remember that when I'm a reporter trying to get to the bottom of a big corporate scandal...maybe by then you will be corrupt enough to share with me."

Stephanie's face goes back to the plastic smile. "That's not how you keep big corporate clients. The most important thing you can do for your client is to keep your mouth shut, or you will lose them. It's serious." Stephanie stares at Addison, as if she is truly protecting an important client, and her loyalty impresses Addison.

"No, I was only kidding, Stephanie, I didn't mean to imply that you would give out trade secrets, honestly. So, will you practice the same type of law?"

"Absolutely. No question in my mind."

"Does your mother support your choice to follow your father's footsteps?"

"My mother's opinion is irrelevant. She left my dad when I was five because he wouldn't spend time with her. She found a new guy who doted on her, only he didn't want a little brat along for the ride. So it's been just me and my dad all these years. That's why I was always in his office — where else would I have gone on the weekends when he had to work? He could have had the nanny watch me, but he knew I wanted to be with him instead. He would

81

find something I could do that made me feel like it was helpful to have me there, rather than the distraction I'm sure that I was."

"What a beautiful story Stephanie."

"It's just Dad and me."

"What about friends and other family, do they have an opinion?"

"Honestly, anyone who has been part of my life knows this is what I want, what I have always wanted. And everyone else, I guess they expect it; and if they don't agree, I really don't care. It's my life, not theirs." Stephanie's closing comment ends the interview perfectly. She is as confident in her choice to follow in her father's footsteps as Mason is in betraying his parents' dream of an Ivy League education and illustrious career, or in Jamison's confidence that he wants to give two years of his life to the Peace Corps, or Monique's desire to pursue a life in theater, regardless of her success, or lack thereof. It is the perfect complement to her story.

"Stephanie, it's been great to interview you today; I appreciate you taking the time. I think your experience will fit perfectly into my story."

"Would you mind if I ask to read the article before it's published? I want to make sure you don't misrepresent me, especially in our conversation about revealing client information. It could be damaging to both my and my father's reputation if you put it out there in an unflattering light."

"Already thinking like a lawyer I see. Yes, I don't mind if you read your portion of the story." Addison doesn't promise to let her read it in its entirety, she doesn't want to give Stephanie the chance to comment on the angle or the other students' views before the rest of the school, but luckily, she either doesn't notice, or isn't concerned about how others appear.

8

It's a Date

Saturday, February 13

Saturday finally arrives, and Addison has been thinking of Mason, even when she knows that she doesn't have time to focus on him. While she is writing, doing Trig problems, working on her APUSH paper, and doing her lab report, he keeps popping into her thoughts. Thankfully this has been a taper week for track, so she's been on short, easy runs, and she has indulged in replaying their interview date at Rocco's, and the meet on Wednesday. She wonders what type of adventure Mason has planned for her today.

He has given her little information: she is supposed to be up early, ready to ride out at 6:30 a.m.; gear needed are hiking shoes or boots, long pants, layers on top, with a fleece coat, hat, and gloves. She checks her phone to see what the temperature is: it's thirty-two now, but a high of fifty-five and sunny. A perfect February day to be doing something outside.

She is awake early because she has butterflies in her stomach. She stays in bed, cuddling with Chandler; it is dark and quiet in her room. Usually she can hear the whirring of the air coming out of the vents, but the fan must have cycled off, and because it is February, there are no birds or bugs to be heard outside of her window. All she can hear is Chandler's slow, even breathing, as he

83

continues to dream of squirrels and rabbits.

At 5:45 her alarm resonates through her bedroom. Despite the fact that the sun won't be up for another hour, the fact that it is Saturday and the fact that she should be in bed well past ten in the morning, she throws back her covers and thrusts her legs over the side of her bed, slipping her feet into her cozy Ugg slippers, which were a gift from her Nanna at Christmas. She doesn't bother with a shower, because she is going to be in a hat most of the day, and somehow she suspects that this adventure won't include a spa day, or a fancy meal out. She slips on a pair of fleece-lined Under Armor tights, pulls on a turtleneck and crew-collared zip-up, and finishes up with her favorite pink North Face fleece. She digs in her drawers for thick, cozy socks, and finds a pink hat that Nanna has knitted for her (sweet Nanna always worries about Addison being cold, and has provided her with warm and cozy clothes each Christmas as long as she can remember). She finds a pair of thick fleece gloves that she shoves into her pockets, along with the hat.

She looks in the mirror; after she washed her face earlier, she only put on sunscreen. Now she decides to add a little color to her eyelids, and a bit of mascara. She can't go on an outdoor adventure fully made up, she wouldn't blame Mason for teasing her if she did. She brushes her hair and puts it in a ponytail. Simple. She considers her reflection; she has managed to look somewhat elegant, despite the five layers of fleece and undergarments.

She makes herself some oatmeal and pours the coffee that her mother has prepared the evening before. She sits at the kitchen table, enjoying the alone time. She is grateful that her mother had the insight not to get up and see her off as if she were still six. However, she doesn't doubt for one second that her mom will be watching from her bedroom window as Mason pulls into the driveway.

Promptly at 6:30, Addison hears tires on the gravel, and puts her bowl and mug in the sink. She grabs the two thermoses of coffee she prepared for the road, hoping that Mason likes it black.

Before she can get to the front door, there is a gentle knock. She opens the door, and Mason is standing on the front porch. He is bundled in his hat, a scarf, a large, thick fleece coat and old worn jeans. He looms in the front door, his head almost reaching the door frame. He is wearing big, heavy leather lumber boots. He looks gruff this early in the morning, with a stubble of a beard, his voice still stiff from lack of use.

"Good morning, girl, ready to go?"

"I made you a coffee to go...black, is that okay?"

"Perfect. Let's hustle, we have a long drive ahead of us."

Addison and Mason climb into his truck, which is already toasty warm from the drive to her house. He has country music playing lightly in the background. It is still dark, both outside and in the cab of the truck. Addison feels as if she and Mason are in their own private world isolated from all the pressure and expectations on the outside. Mason pulls the car out of the driveway and is focusing on the road. It gives her a few minutes to look at him, without him really noticing. The dash lights illuminate his face, and she studies his profile. His nose and chin are the most prominent features, they give him a look of strength and power. His nose is straight and long. It has a strong angular bridge, and almost looks sculpted in its straightness, except for a little bump in the middle of his nose. She wonders if he has broken his nose somehow. His strong jaw bone leads to a dimpled chin. She wonders how he manages to shave right in the center of that dimple.

"What you looking at, Addison?" Mason looks at her sideways, trying to keep his eye on the road. He is grinning at her, his face showing evidence of trying to keep a straight face, but fails miserably.

"Honestly, I was wondering how you shave that dimple in the tip of your chin."

"Ha...well, hence the day-old beard today. I hate shaving my chin. I hate shaving in general, but especially my chin. I've thought of growing a goatee, but somehow, the image doesn't really go with high school junior. I think my mother would throw me out of the house."

"I can imagine. I kind of like the scruffy look you have going on today." Addison feels like she's revealed too much, so she quickly directs the conversation back to safe zone. "So, where is our adventure taking us?" She holds her mug in both her hands, letting the aroma of her hazelnut coffee waft through the air, making the cab seem even cozier.

"You have to wait, not revealing my secrets yet." Now his grin is even more obvious; he has stopped even trying to hide the fact that he is smiling and enjoying himself.

"So not fair!"

"I will tell you that I'm taking you to one of my favorite places on Earth." As he says this, he reaches across the seat and grabs her hand, which now lies in her lap. She feels a bolt of electricity run from the top of her hand, where his covers hers, to the back of her neck, and all the way down her spine. Her stomach immediately responds by first dropping down to what feels like the floor, and then bouncing right back to her throat. She can't believe that one touch from his hand on hers can affect her so, the hand that has touched probably thousands of people throughout her life, yet not a single one of them has had the same effect on her. She is a little self-conscious, a little nervous about him holding her hand. "I don't take many people out there. In fact, I have never taken a girl before."

"Well, then I'm honored. I can't wait to see where it's."

At 6:45, the sun to meet the horizon behind them, at the same time as Mason steers the car onto Highway 66 West, leading them out of McLean and outside of the beltway, the freeway which encompasses Washington, D.C. and its immediate suburbs. Beyond the beltway are the never-ending suburbs, which span forty-five miles outside of the city, all through Virginia and Maryland in a large circle. Route 66 West is a straight shot, starting right next to the Kennedy Center, through Arlington and west, until it ends in the foothills of the Shenandoah Mountains. The distant mountains can almost be mistaken for dark clouds. But to those native to Virginia, they know they are there. As the pick-up crosses over the beltway, the sun moves its way up into the sky; the day is clear. The light is warm, brightening the surroundings as they drive. In the distance, the Blue Ridge Mountains are visible; a line of mountains looming on the horizon, a hazy blue, jagged line full of a promise of adventure.

Mason and Addison talk comfortably throughout the drive. They share stories about growing up, their parents, and how different they are. Both Mason and Addison are only children, so they share the experience of being alone, and entertaining themselves. They are both fiercely independent as a result. The conversation lapses into comfortable silences, followed by an influx of questions and stories.

They talk about embarrassing moments that they can't live down. Addison learns that Mason has two sets of friends: one from his childhood and the country, whom he sees on the weekends and during the summer; and another group from McLean, a much smaller group of friends who share interests in hunting and the outdoors. His two groups mingle sometimes when he brings his McLean friends out to Marshall. However, his Marshall friends have never come into McLean before. They hate the city, they don't like the traffic they have to travel through, and they hold their own stereotypical biases against the snobby rich kids they think Mason hangs out with, and to some degree, has become.

He tells her of his friends in Marshall, in particular his best friend, Beckett, who lives one farm over. They've known each other since before they can even remember. As he tells her all about his childhood and friends, she finds herself longing to meet his friends, and his parents.

Addison shares stories about being alone frequently, having to find ways to entertain herself when her parents were busy or traveling. When she was little, she had a nanny because, despite the fact that her mom worked from home in her studio, she needed time to concentrate. Not only that, but when her mother was focused on her artwork, she was so focused, she wouldn't have heard Addison, even if she were next to her, screaming for help. So, the nanny cared for her when her mom worked, and stayed at their house when her parents traveled. Her mother did, and still has, art shows all over the country, New York, San Francisco, Miami, and would attend artist retreats in Sante Fe and Boulder. During those times, Addison was lonely and would imagine different adventures she would experience when she was grown, like traveling and exploring the mysteries of the world. Now she is at the precipice, almost ready to jump into the world of her future. She is ready to start her adventures, to make those dreams and fantasies a reality. She can't wait to graduate and go to college.

They continue down 66, passing all the suburbs. The distance between the houses and towns grows wider with every mile until they are surrounded by the rolling hills that are typical of Virginian countryside. This is now horse country, with small fields divided by lines of trees or rocks. Large homes are nestled against the hills, and barns accompany most of the homes. It is a cold early morning, so there are no animals to be seen on the drive out, but Addison hopes she is able to catch sight of some horses on the way back. The sun is now fully up in the east and is focused on the mountain range ahead of them. The foothills, which they are driving through, are a dark green, set against the blue of the mountains in the distance.

"Are we there yet? This is really going to be an all-day event, isn't it?"

"It is. Remind me of your curfew again?" Addison can hear the smile in his voice, even as she is focused on the scenery outside of her window. They are passing the ruins of a mill which was built along Bull Run, a small "run" or creek, which runs from the mountains towards Manassas, and which was the site of the first battle of the Civil War. It is breathtakingly beautiful, and simultaneously sad, seeing such a big and beautiful building standing in ruins.

"I should probably be home by midnight, not necessarily because it's my curfew, which it is, but because I can't imagine I will have enough energy to keep going much past that, with this early morning adventure."

"I promise you this, you will be tired by the time I drop you off tonight. But you will be really happy that you came."

As they pass the exit for Marshall, Mason slows the car down, and points at the hills to the left of the highway. "See that hill right there, to the left, with the yellow farmhouse right up against the bottom of the hill?"

"Yes," Addison looks to the left, and sees a large foothill, with fields along the base of the hill, and thick trees rounding the top of the hill. Against the blue mountains, it looks like a scene that you could have come across two-hundred years ago. The faded yellow farmhouse is nestled into the side of the hill, making it almost appear tucked in. There is a red barn to the right of it. From this distance she can see the enormity of the property and its outbuildings.

"Those fields at the bottom are part of our farm, and the hill is where my dad and I hunt, and we fell the trees, too, for extra lumber."

"It looks lovely. How big is the farm?"

"It's about 300 acres. But we own another farm about the same size that my dad bought right around the time that I was born, and he has another smaller farm, about 100 acres that he uses mostly to grow hay for the horses and cattle."

"That sounds like an awful lot of acreage. I don't have a clue what a good size farm would be. I know that my mom has stayed on a ranch in New Mexico, where she was painting, and it was about 3000 acres. I have no idea if that is a lot, or little."

"Well, for places like New Mexico, Idaho, Wyoming, you'll have acreages like that. They have ranches, and they run their herds on that land; they don't use it to farm as much as to feed their livestock. In Virginia, the average farm is probably closer to 150 acres. Like I told you at Rocco's, my dad has done well for himself by buying up farms when the market was low. He bought neighboring smaller farms so he could make a big farm. Some of the land isn't as farmable, because it's hilly, but we love it for hunting and four-wheeling, plus my dad loves to build furniture during the winters, so he plants trees up there that he can use for his furniture, like cherry and walnut. He's always looking for a way for the farm to keep providing money for the family."

"So, you own a lot of land in terms of Virginia, but a tiny bit if you lived in New Mexico. Funny how location makes all the difference. It seems like anything on the East Coast is expensive: land, food, cars, taxes. All of it."

"I feel another story coming on. I can see you writing about the unfair pricing for those living on the East Coast."

"Don't even get me started. I already have so much to write, I'll hold off on that one for a little while."

They continue to drive, and Addison is surprised that the farm is not the destination, she thought that they might be headed there. Now she is really intrigued and curious. They have ridden in the car for almost ninety minutes.

Mason pulls the car onto the exit ramp at highway 647, a two lane highway traveling from 66 West towards the Shenandoah

Valley.

"Are we going hiking by chance?"

"Shoot. You figured it out! But, there are over a 500 miles of trails in the Shenandoah alone. You have no idea where we are actually heading."

Addison only knows of a few hikes in the park, and she has only heard of them, she's never hiked them herself. "I guess I will wait and see, because I don't have a clue."

"What I can say is that I'm taking you to the most breathtaking view in the world today. You are one lucky girl."

"I literally can't wait. Like really. My bottom and legs are numb."

"Sit tight for about another thirty minutes. Want a snack? I packed some Cliff Bars, trail mix and peanut butter sandwiches, and some fruit too," says Mason as he reaches for his cooler in the back and hands it to her.

"I'd love a Cliff Bar, thank you!"

"Help yourself. Save some for our hike."

"Will you tell me how far we're going?"

"The hike takes the average person five hours, but most athletes can do it in three. I figured we'd go fast, but take a break at the top for an early lunch."

After twenty-five more minutes, following increasingly smaller roads and into even smaller towns they pull into a small parking lot for Old Rag. The sign outside the Ranger's hut indicates that it is the most popular, and most challenging hike in Shenandoah National Park. They pack up their backpacks with food and water, and head to the official trailhead. The start of the hike is actually a steep road that leads to the trailhead.

It is now about 8:30, and the air is crisp and cold. There is still frost along the trail, making the rocks slick, and the trees are covered in a white layer of icing creating a winter wonderland. Addison hopes that this hike won't injure her as she slips on a rock on the trail. She wishes Mason had asked her first; a long hike isn't the best tapering before the conference meet. She considers that if Mason had been an athlete groomed for success, he would never have taken her on a hike with such a grueling reputation. At the same time, it is beautiful, and she has Mason to herself for the day.

She decides that she wants to live life in the now, rather than only preparing for the future, and pushes her doubts to the back of her mind.

Once they hit the official trailhead, they start out on a rocky path with a small incline, running through a pine forest. The forest floor is covered with a thick layer of pine needles. The ground is moist under the pine needles and the forest gives off a deep rich scent of pine trees and fertile earth which smells of musk and leaves. Roots and rocks peek out from beneath the earth and pine needles, making it necessary to step carefully as they hike. As the path progresses and they climb further up the mountain. The trees thin out and the path becomes more technical, eventually becoming mostly rocky cliffs that she and Mason scramble up.

They are moving at a fast clip, and despite their heavy breathing, they banter lively the entire hike up, sometimes teasing one another, sometimes discussing serious topics, and sometimes being quiet. At ten-thirty they make it up to the top of Old Rag. The top of the mountain is made up of slabs of granite, slanted so that hikers can sit on the slabs almost as if leaning back in a recliner. The view from Old Rag is incredible. Addison and Mason rotate and can see 365 degrees of the Shenandoah Valley around them. The mountain is so high that the view to the bottom is almost hazy despite it being a cloudless day. The sun has warmed the rocks making the granite comfortable to sit on. They pull out their sandwiches and water bottles and sit down to look over the valley.

Mason glances over at Addison as they unwrap their peanut butter sandwiches. "I can't believe how good peanut butter and jelly tastes when you're really hungry."

Addison nods, because she has a mouth full of bread. She swallows, "It's the best meal I've ever had. How could I be so hungry at only ten-thirty?"

"Guess hiking and talking is just that awesome."

"So much for tapering."

"Whoops. I hadn't thought of that. We shot-putters don't really need to taper all that much, and I'm new to this whole track thing anyway, so I didn't even consider that this was not the best idea for you. I'm really sorry."

"It's worth it. I mean, look at this view. I wouldn't have missed it for anything. The company isn't bad either." She looks at Mason, but this time, she isn't holding back with a shy glance. She has had an amazing time, and she feels a strong connection to Mason. She really can't remember a time when she has been happier or more content, and she wants him to know it. "This has been a special day, Mason; thank you for bringing me up here."

"I was hoping that you would like it as much as I do. You don't find folks who enjoy a difficult hike every day. I thought you might like the exercise, and I was really hoping that you'd love the view as much as I do."

"I do, it's breathtaking. It's almost surreal...it looks like a postcard, or a painting."

Mason reaches for her hand a second time that morning and holds on tight. Her stomach flips again, and the heat rushes from his hand all the way through her body once again. She wonders if his kiss would have the same effect on her.

As if on cue, he leans towards her, looking her in the eyes, then slowly closes his eyes, and he gently places his lips on hers. The flood of electricity that rushes through her body is incredible. Her entire being responds to his kiss; she has never experienced anything like this before.

When she was freshman, she went to homecoming with Andrew Beardsley; he kissed her at the end of the date. They had gone with a group, and right before her parents picked them up from the dance, he had pulled her into a corner and clumsily kissed her. It had been more teeth and head butting than kissing, and she only remembers feeling distracted and grossed out by him. He had been sweaty, and his lips were like a little boy's, with peach fuzz grazing his upper lip. She had wondered if there was anything wrong with her, why she had not responded to his kiss. The opportunity to test her kissing response had never again presented itself, and she had continued on to this moment, wondering why everyone was so crazy about kissing. Until now.

This kiss, her first real kiss, is the antithesis of that kiss. Mason has a scruffy beard that gently scrapes her lips. He kisses her with a confidence that demonstrates that he is more man than boy. His right hand moves to her shoulder, causing more waves of electrical shock to move through her. His other hand slips on to her hip where it stays for the duration of the kiss.

When they finally part, both are breathless. She has no words to express her reaction to him, so she simply looks into his eyes, and then sits closer to his side and leans into his shoulder. In anticipation, Mason already has his arm ready to wrap around her shoulder. They sit together like this, looking over the valley for a long time, feeling comfortable and close.

Eventually neither the heat from their bodies nor the continually rising sun is warm enough. They need to start moving again. "We should head back down the mountain. I want to take you out for dinner. If we don't leave now, we won't be able to eat before it gets too crowded. Besides, my butt has frozen to the granite."

"Yeah, I'm freezing. Is it the same hike back?"

"No, we go back on the other side, and it's much easier, no scrambling."

"Good, because I couldn't make it down those cliffs without injuring myself, and Coach would have your hide."

They head down the mountain passing through switchbacks, and eventually making it to a wide path with an easy decline. When they finally make it back to the car, it is almost already two in the afternoon. They are warmed up now and wrap their fleece jackets around their waists. By the time they get to the car, the sun is already starting its decline, and it is getting chillier again. Addison shrugs on her coat, they knock the dirt off their boots and climb back into the truck.

"I'm so tired. That was a great hike, but it's long!"

"Did you work up an appetite?"

"Yup, I'm starving again. Do you mind if I have a banana to tide me over?"

"Help yourself."

Mason starts the truck, and it comes to life with the deep rhythm of the diesel engine. Its rumble is somehow reassuring to Addison, just as Mason's presence is. She is amazed once again how close she feels to Mason, especially after only a week of getting to know him. She wonders if there is something to the idea of soulmates. Can a person really meet someone and have an instant connection because they were meant to be together? Or, do some people click more than others for no reason other than that their personalities fit? When she first met Campbell, they also had an instant connection. She had felt that they had always known each other, that their friendship had somehow carried over from some other part of her life. She still can't explain it, yet she is feeling the same type of connection with Mason, but tenfold.

"A penny for your thoughts."

"I was thinking about destiny. Do you think we all have a destiny we're meant to fulfil, or do you believe that it's all` free will and random?"

"Well, I sure feel like I was destined to meet you, if that's what you mean." How had he read her mind so perfectly? Yes, she did have an immediate connection to Mason, she did believe that they were meant to meet, that this feeling she has is the fulfillment of a plan for her. It's so odd, because similarly Addison has always felt an innate destiny to be a journalist, and maybe she is also meant to be with Mason. At least in this part of her life.

"Well, I didn't think I believed in destiny, but I'm quickly becoming a believer." She smiles and settles into her seat. She looks out of the window, as the beautiful countryside passes, and Mason reaches for her hand again, only this time she isn't self-conscience of his touch, and she enjoys the warm, comforting sensation that his hand gives her.

"Would you like the Mason Gentry tour of Virginia, Part I?"

"Sure. What's Part I, and how many parts are there?"

"Well, Part I would be the area we drove through this morning, only we will cover it in more detail this afternoon, ending with a fabulous dinner in Front Royal."

The scenery is incredible. Mason seems to know all the small country roads. They pass through tiny towns that are only a few buildings long, but all containing adorable old homes and shops. Most of the homes bordering the country roads have front porches that overlook not only the traffic as it slowly passes by, but also the hollows and ridges they are nestled in.

Between the small towns are both large and small farms. Most farms have a manor house and barns. In typical Virginian style, the fields are separated by fences made of stones that the farmers have pulled from their fields. Horses and cattle are grazing in the warm February afternoon sun. The two-lane country roads rise and dip with the hills, and the effect is a lulling rhythm which makes Addison feel even more comfortable with Mason, their conversation flowing naturally.

Mason drives through the winding roads, showing Addison all the different places he has visited in his childhood, from Civil War memorials, to picnics and little league games. He explains that when you live in the country you expect to travel a half hour to an hour for activities, which limits the activities that parents can get their children to. It also means that Mason has traveled all through the area over the course of the years.

After several hours of driving and explanations, Mason pulls back onto Stonewall Jackson Highway. They fall into a comfortable silence and the truck travels north towards Front Royal.

Addison wakes up with a start. It is dark outside, and the truck has stopped moving. She guesses that is what woke her up. She sits up, feeling confused. She sees Mason looking over at her, with that silly grin on his face again.

"Well, hello, Sleeping Beauty. Did you enjoy your little nap?"

Addison quickly touches her chin and cheek to make sure she wasn't drooling. How embarrassing to fall asleep like a little girl. She feels humiliated.

"I'm so sorry, that is so embarrassing. I can't believe I did that! I guess it was a busy week, and that hike took more out of me than I thought it would."

"Don't be embarrassed. You were so peaceful and beautiful in your sleep; you looked like an angel. I'm really glad you were able to sleep. Maybe even a little jealous."

"Where are we?" Addison stretches as she becomes fully awake. They are parked in a small parking lot in front of a little restaurant.

"This is Blue Wing Frog. It's one of my favorite places to eat. It's quirky, has good food, a nice location, and casual enough for a couple of hikers."

"Well, good, I'm starving!"

Mason opens the door for Addison, making her feel like they have stepped back in time. "After you, Angel."

"Angel?"

"Yup, after sleeping like an angel, that has become your new identity in my mind."

When they walk into the restaurant, a young hostess greets them, "Hey, Mason, nice to see you."

"Hey Susan — good to see you. Could we have a table for two?"

"Seat yourself. Take a pick, as you can see."

The restaurant is almost empty, with an older couple sitting near the front, and a young mother and her two children about midway into the restaurant. In the center of the restaurant is a giant sized picnic table, big enough for Paul Bunyan to sit at.

"What is that thing?"

"I told you it was a quirky place. They love to embrace the weirdness in life."

Mason and Addison choose a table near the back of the restaurant. They slide in opposite of each other.

"You come here often enough to be recognized?"

"Well, your choices of hip hangouts in Marshall aren't all that many, so we come to Front Royal whenever we want 'city life,' as my friends like to call it. Susan actually lives pretty close to me, and this is a good gig for her. It's not a large crowd you see on a Saturday at five, but this place is pretty hopping towards seven. Most of the 'cool' couples come here. But five o'clock is more the blue hair special, and great for young families, since the old folks are too deaf to be bothered by the screaming." As if on cue, one of the small children with the young mom bursts out in a vicious scream, as his older brother steals his toy car.

Addison looks over the menu and sees crazy meals and menu items. They decide to order the appetizer, 'Nibbly Bits Platter'; Mason orders the 'Death by Pork' sandwich, and Addison orders the 'Pomegranate Chicken' sandwich. They also order two micro-brewed sodas.

"This place is so cool. I can't imagine such a quirky place in McLean."

"We don't take ourselves too seriously out here in the

country. Yep, got to be able to make fun of yourself, enjoy life, and embrace the weirdness." Somehow Mason's Southern accent, his Virginia country twang, is stronger out here. She wonders if he represses his accent to fit into McLean more.

"I suppose so, it's really pretty refreshing, honestly. Sometimes, I get swept up in the pressure, the list of accomplishments I need to achieve, and how everything I do will add to my resume and my college application. I get so busy running from one event to the next that I don't even get to stop and think about what it all means. This has been a great break from my crazy."

"You should take more breaks from your crazy. Maybe you really should consider how much all that really matters in the long run. Does it really matter if you get into Columbia? Maybe there's another school that can give you the same quality of education, but one that won't expect you to sacrifice every moment of your life to get in. Not only that, but have you thought about what it might be like for you when you do make it in? If they want all this from you to be accepted into their program, what might they expect from you once you're in?"

"I believe that if I don't get into Columbia, my opportunities as a journalist will be so limited. New York is where the action is, the connections through Columbia will land me an internship which will lead to a job." Just discussing it is making Addison's anxiety level go up. She panics when she considers what her life might be like without Columbia.

"The other schools that are even close to being as good as Columbia are in the boonies. University of Bloomington in Indiana, Northwestern University, and then there is UNC Chapel Hill, they are a little easier to get into than Columbia, but they are so far from New York — where all the news action is. Columbia has been my dream for so long. I want it."

"I guess I'm more focused on the after, so the schooling isn't as important to me. I know I need college to be successful, and I know that Virginia Tech will be a good fit for me, but if I end up having to go somewhere else, it's okay with me. I'm sure as heck not going to run myself ragged to get in."

"The difference is that you already own a farm and have a

certain future waiting for you. You don't need to think of connections who might want to hire you down the road. You are hiring yourself. You already don't have to answer to anyone but yourself. I envy that."

"Well, I do have to answer to the market, and I need to make and keep good relationships with my buyers, but you're right; my dad has set it all up for me, and as long as I don't act like a complete idiot, I should be able to make it. Have you considered being a freelancer when you graduate and letting your work speak for itself? Once a few really good, strong stories run, people won't care where you were educated, they will care about the quality of your stories."

"And in the meantime? What if it takes me a year or two, or even five to build that reputation? How do I feed myself?"

"Won't your dad help you get on your feet?"

"He already doesn't think I can make a career out of writing. It would make him right, and I would rather die than help him prove himself right. I want to be wildly successful so that my dream is legitimate."

"I guess that will depend on how you plan on defining 'wildly successful' and whether your father will agree with you."

"Maybe you're right, maybe there is no pleasing Daddy anyway. Maybe I need to think about what's going to make me happy. I know I want to travel the world, and I know that I want to make a difference." Addison sits quietly, thinking about what would really make her happy in life. Is it travel? Is it making a difference in the world? If that is it, she would never be able to spend her life with someone like Mason. He wants Virginia; he is tied to the land. She is the opposite. She feels no roots to home. She can't wait to spread her wings and leave. The realization makes her sad in a strange sort of way. Like mourning the loss of something you don't even have yet.

"What's wrong? Did I push too much?" Mason looks concerned as he gazes at her. She is visibly distracted and withdrawn.

"It dawned on me that we want polar opposites from life..." The rest of the sentence isn't spoken. They both know that it means that there is no point in pursuing a relationship that has no future. Or is it? Addison is always so focused on her end goals, her future. Should she be?

"Or, we could enjoy each other's company and see where life ends up taking us. Maybe our futures are much more fluid than you think. Maybe there's a plan for each of us that neither you nor I have even dreamt up. I will tell you what, I certainly won't worry about it at seventeen. I enjoy our time together, and I'm pretty sure that you do too. That's all I'm going to worry about for now."

"I'm sure that I will end up worrying for us both then. I seem to excel in that department."

After they finish their meals, they order the 'Kat Cake', a chocolate and raspberry cake, rich and deliciously decadent. They dive into it together, almost fighting each other for the choicest pieces.

"I think I might enjoy your appetite as much as I enjoy our conversation. It's really refreshing to see a girl house her food like you do!"

Addison laughs. "Are you calling me a pig?"

"Piglet would be more appropriate."

"Well, we hiked four hours. What did you expect?"

"I expect you to eat exactly what you did. I think most girls secretly eat in private and then pick at their food in public. I don't know how else they would survive on the food they consume in public."

When the waitress comes by, Mason hands her cash for their meal. He then looks back at Addison, "Would you like to continue your Mason Gentry Tour of Virginia? I'd love to take you through Marshall, even though it'll be dark."

"Is there even anything to see out here when it's dark?"

"Not really, but I will take you through our tiny little town, and if you play your cards right, I will drive you past the main farm and house. But no, we are not stopping at the house. I'm not ready to unleash Mamma Gentry on you yet."

"Sounds good, I don't think I'm ready to meet your mom, but I would like to see where you grew up."

They drive another half an hour until they reach Marshall. Downtown Marshall is small, and now that it is dark, it looks cozy, with small old buildings, and the lights burning inside the homes along the main street.

After visiting town, they head south along Highway 55 and turn off on a small country road. Addison can see the shadows of the stone fences they have seen all day long. They take another turn, and are now on an even smaller road.

"Look to the right there....do you see the stone pillars?"

Mason slows down the car so she can see the letters on the pillar: Aberdale Farm. There is an iron gate.

"It's called Aberdale Farm? I love that name!"

"This is the original farm that my great-great-grandparents started. Then my grandparents took it over and raised my dad on the farm. When they retired, my father bought them out. They moved into town, and we moved in here. The house was built in 1827. The original building was a small and basic farm house, but each generation added more to it. My parents added the sunroom, the pagoda and a lot of the landscaping when they took over the farm. You can't see the house from here well, but if you look down the driveway, you can see it in the distance."

"This is incredible, Mason." Addison looks down the driveway, through the gates, and can see a light yellow manor home nestled into the hill behind it. She can see some of the windows lit from the inside. "Are your parents there now?"

"Yeah, they spend their weekends there, and often my dad is out here during the week to manage the workers, and I think he really loves being out here. My mom has been staying with me in McLean most days. But there are days when she comes out here too, and I hang out by myself, or go stay with a friend. Most weekends I'm home with my parents, working the farm."

"I can't wait to see it in daylight someday. I really hadn't expected such a beautiful home."

"Okay, Angel, I got to get you home, and I think we both need some rest."

Addison thinks to herself that she likes it when he calls her Angel. It makes her feel special and precious.

They drive the remaining hour home, chatting about the farm, the hike and enjoying a comfortable silence together.

9
Broadening Horizons
Sunday, February 14

Sunday morning Addison wakes up, tired, but feeling content. She relives her adventures from the day before. When Mason brought her home at nine, he had parked the truck at the end of the driveway, and she had gotten her second kiss from him. It had been equally thrilling as the Old Rag kiss, but it had been more relaxed and comfortable this time, and longer.

Mason had walked her to the front door, where her mother, father and Chandler had been waiting, and Mason had politely introduced himself and, thankfully, had begged off with the excuse that he had to get up early in the morning.

Her father had responded much more calmly than she had expected. Mason's Southern politeness had helped to assuage him. She could also tell that her father was tired himself, and that had probably added to his calmness. He had requested that she eat breakfast with the family and attend church together.

Addison can smell the coffee and can hear her mother and father moving around in the kitchen. She is not quite ready to face her family yet, so she grabs her phone off the bedside table and sees that she has a text from Campbell: *what's going on? Scoop please!* How much should she share with Campbell? She is her best friend, but right now, Addison loves that yesterday is a memory that she and Mason alone share. She wouldn't want him telling his buddies. On the other hand, she's also dying to relive parts of the day by sharing. She decides to keep it as private as she can.

An amazing day.

Details?

Let's say that the day was perfect, and I can't wait to see him again.

Jamison and a bunch of us are going out this evening for Valentine's Day. Do you want to check if Mason wants to come?

Hanging out with Mason would be wonderful. She would love to have him to herself, but she also wants to spend time with Campbell, and she loved talking with Jamison. Plus, she can observe how Mason acts when he's around other people. It's always good to get a second opinion, and she values Campbell's.

Sure, I'll ask him. What time, where?

No idea. I'll text you when J gets back to me.

Next, she texts Mason. Part of her is afraid she isn't playing "hard to get" by waiting for Mason to text her, but at the same time, she hates games; if he wants to play games she doesn't want any part of it. She moves onto her next dilemma. Should tell him Happy Valentine's Day….it would be so awkward after only having been on one date. She doesn't want to make him feel like he is supposed to do something special for her. She decides to ignore it.

Good morning. Yesterday was great. Campbell, Jamison and a group of us are hanging out tonight. Wanna?

She doesn't want to lay in bed knowing her invitation is floating out there in cyberspace. The problem with texting is that the sender never knows when the receiver gets it, if they are choosing not to respond immediately, or if they haven't read it yet. He had said that he had to get up early and is probably at the farm, feeding horses or cleaning stalls. She isn't going to worry about it, and decides to get up and join her family for breakfast.

"Hey, Daddy," Addison says, walking into the cheery kitchen. Like the rest of the house, the kitchen is bright, with a French influence. Light yellow walls, white cabinets, and a cozy breakfast nook overlooking the garden. Derrick Erhard is standing at the center island, where he is frying bacon on the Viking stove. Her mother is next to him cutting fruit.

The tension Addison is so familiar with is an unwelcome guest in the kitchen. Despite the fact that this is her father's only day away from work, and there is no bank business, no crisis and no meetings and Dad can hang out with the family, there is always the underlying unresolved issue. The difference with today is that Addison knows what it is now. She understands the tension. She looks at her parents as they work alongside each other preparing breakfast. She is struck with the cruelty of it. Clearly her parents had a love for each other that caused her mother to give in to her father's plan, but she hasn't learned to have peace with that decision. To bear that cross for all these years, to never accept it, must have eaten away at her mother, and at her love for Addison's father.

It is rare in this day and age for couples to be together long and to remain happy; especially in McLean, where business and social obligations often take priority over family. She isn't sure how her parents' marriage has lasted despite it all, other than they share their love for her. She wonders if her mother would finally be at peace if they sold the house and had a fresh start; or would their lives always be tainted by Pop's indiscretion? It seems unfair to Addison. Her father has made an honest living; he has worked hard to rebuild what Pop almost destroyed. She looks at her father with admiration.

"How is my princess this morning?"

"I'm a little sore, I'm not gonna lie. I'm a little worried about the meet on Friday. Hopefully there's enough time to recover before then."

"Was it a good decision to hike yesterday? Maybe you should have considered that… Conferences are a big deal, Addison."

"I know they are, Dad. I wasn't aware of the plan — because it was a surprise. I didn't know how hard the hike would be. Mason didn't realize that I needed to be tapering, not climbing."

"It sounds to me as if he doesn't have your best interests in mind, or he would have checked with you."

Her mother jumps in, as she always does, redirecting the conversation to safer waters, "Well, honey, was it worth it? Did you and Mason get a chance to talk and learn about each other?"

"Yes, it was wonderful. We talked the entire drive and the whole hike up and down — all eight miles. It was breathtakingly beautiful up there."

"Well, you know I think that life experiences and adventures are far more valuable than material accomplishments. I'm happy you went and had a good time."

Her father isn't convinced, "So, tell me more about this Mason. Mom says that he lives out in the country? He wants to be a farmer? How did you meet him? Where is he applying to schools? Who are his parents?"

"Whoa with the ninth-degree, Daddy. Let me drink a cup of coffee before I give you his resume!"

Grabbing her favorite coffee cup, a light pastel ceramic mug her mother made in her studio, Addison pours herself a cup of coffee and adds some cream. She sits herself at the island, Chandler following her every move, and finally settles himself under Addison's stool after several pointless circles in the effort to find the correct patch of light. She starts telling her father all about how she met Mason, his dream to take over the family farm and convert it to organic-only produce, and his split life between McLean and Marshall. To his credit, her dad listens quietly, asking a few clarifying questions, and lets her finish. Her mother continues to make pancakes, quietly listening along, but leaving the conversation for Addison and her father.

"Well, he seems like an okay guy, other than the fact that he wants to be an organic farmer. I don't understand why he would pass up on the opportunity his father has provided for him to live a better life. Although, in my opinion you are doing the same. Choosing a career which isn't guaranteed to make you successful, and frankly one which is beneath your abilities and social class."

"Daddy, that's exactly what draws us together; we both want to follow our dreams, to become who *we* want to be, even if society and our parents don't buy into it. It's our choice as independent human beings to choose our life path."

"It is, only as long as you can support yourself. I have a hard time believing that you aren't going to be knocking on my door asking for some help getting on your feet, which I will happily do, but I will say 'I told you so.' But that is another conversation. Regarding Mason, where could this relationship with him possibly go? You want to travel the world, and he will be busy mucking out stalls."

"Can we not do this now? This is making my head hurt, I had a nice day, and now you're making one date about my entire life. I went on *one* date, Dad. Can we let the future wait another day?"

"Okay, I will let it go for now, Addison, but we are not finished discussing your future. We never will be, it's our biggest concern and our job, frankly, to prepare you for a successful adult life."

"Addie, could you pour us all orange juice? Derrick, could you please bring the bacon and sausage to the breakfast table? Let's sit down and enjoy our breakfast. We've got about an hour before we need to leave for church."

The rest of breakfast is spent discussing Derrick's work week, projects that her mother is working on and Addison's conference meet and her assignments for school. When she goes back to her bedroom to prepare for church, she sees the text she was waiting for: *Love to hang out with the gang; it gives me another excuse to see you again. Ill be back in McLean by 530. Will that be too late?*

Addison responds: *Text me when u r back and ill tell u where to meet.*

The family attends St. John's Episcopal Church on Georgetown Pike. The original church was moved to McLean in 1910 and has been a pillar in the community since. Her father's family has been attending this church since it was moved, and the Erhards always sit in the first pew, where kneeling cushions with the initials of relatives lay on the floor for prayer. She always looks for her great-grandfather's cushion, 'DRE 1916-2003'. Her father is the third in the line of Derrick Ronald Erhard.

Addison sits in their pew with a heavy heart today. Her father has raised issues she knows, deep down, are real. She doubts again whether she can be successful as a journalist if she doesn't attend Columbia; and even if she does, will she ever be successful enough for her father to approve of her choice? What is she going to do about Mason? She loves spending time with him, but they have vastly different dreams and aspirations. She can't see a future as it stands now. Part of her wants to live for the moment, but Addison is a planner, she is seriously focused on her future and she doesn't like to waste time. Is spending time with Mason pointless if she knows it won't go anywhere long term? She spends the church sermon thinking about all of this, and by the end of the service, she is more indecisive, and she's feeling her anxiety and the pressure to make decisions weighing heavily on her.

After church, Addison tackles her work. She finishes her article, and sends it to William to be edited. Between her reading and math assignments, she is busy for most of the afternoon. Around four, Campbell finally texts her: *We r meeting at Tyson's at 630. We r gonna eat and catch a movie. Wanna meet early so we can talk? I can pick you up.*

Addison texts back: *let me check with mason.* She texts Mason: *We r meeting at 6 at Tysons. Wanna go?*

Within a moment, her phone vibrates: *Sure Angel. pick u up at 6?* Now she knows that he is as excited to see her as she is him.

Perfect. She considers saying that she is excited, but she doesn't want to seem overeager.

She messages Campbell back: *Mason is picking me up. meet u at B&N entrance, main level.*

She runs downstairs to tell her mother the plan. Her mother gives her a stern look. "You know your daddy will want him to come to the door and shake hands, like a proper gentleman. He will not look kindly upon him pulling up and you jumping in that truck. He already has his reservations about this boy.

She quickly texts Mason again: *Could u come early? come up to the house. my dad wants to interrogate u.*

Mason pulls into the driveway, and Addison is guessing that he wishes she would meet at the mall instead of coming up to the door and being questioned and intimidated by her father. Her father is sitting in his library, right off the foyer, pretending to work, so he can be the one to open the door. Addison waits in the window seat in the sitting room, perched on the edge, knowing that poor Mason is about to be catechized.

Mason knocks on the door, and Addison watches through the window; he is relaxed and ready for the onslaught. She tries to catch his eye so that she can show him that she is sorry, but he is focused on the door.

"Yes?" Addison's father's voice booms lower and louder than usual. Addison suspects this is the voice with which he handles his employees with, probably when they disappoint him.

"Good evening, Mr. Erhard," he graciously offers his hand. "Nice to meet you." Her father shakes his hand and looks Mason in the eyes. "I would like to take Addison out so she and I can join some of our friends for dinner tonight, with your permission, sir." Mason easily meets her father's eyes, showing confidence and respect. As Addison chooses this moment to walk into the foyer. The scene reminds her of two stags facing off on a Discovery Channel nature show: each staring the other down to show who is in charge.

"Hi, Mason." She stands next to him, to give him as much support as she can, and so she can show her father how comfortable she is with Mason. Her father looks at her over his reading glasses, his dark brows furrowed over his green eyes. He looks at Addison, then looks at Mason again. He clearly is unhappy about the fact that his little girl is going out with this seventeen-year-old 'boy' who doesn't appear any part boy, but all man.

"That depends, young man. Where do you plan on taking my daughter?" Her father asks with an emphasis on the word 'daughter.'

"Yes, sir. We are planning on meeting a group of friends at Tyson's Mall and eating at Coastal Flats. If it's okay with you, I would also like to take her to see a movie with the group." Addison is immensely relieved that her father hasn't asked which movie they are seeing. She would be horrified to have him decide whether a movie is inappropriate for her. At seventeen she feels she has earned the right to make these types of decisions for herself.

"All right, but I expect her home by eleven on a school night, and that's already pushing it." He crosses his arms over his sizable chest, and the intimidation he has planned is evident, and effective. Addison hopes that Mason doesn't actually disappoint her father at some point, or clearly things are going to be unpleasant.

Mason and Addison climb into his truck and head towards Tyson's Corner. Even on a Sunday evening, traffic is horrible in McLean and in the Tyson's area. It takes them a full twenty-five minutes to make the two-mile drive, and they arrive at the Barnes and Noble entrance of the mall just as Campbell, Jamison and a small group of kids from school arrive. Addison recognizes William in the group, walking alongside Jamison and Campbell. She is looking forward to spending time with William outside of school and the journalism late nights.

In typical Campbell fashion, she has called ahead, and when they get to Coastal Flats, a table for ten is ready for them. The group orders appetizers and meals. Mason sits between Addison and Jamison, with William on the other side of Jamison. Addison is relieved that they are talking comfortably. She hears them discussing her article; the Peace Corps and farming, as well as track and running. Jamison isn't on the track team, but he does run cross country, and can be seen running along Chain Bridge Road and Georgetown Pike almost daily, especially early in the morning.

In the meantime, Addison and Campbell talk quietly about her date with Mason. Campbell seems excited, if a little confused about Addison's attraction to Mason. "I mean, I've never seen you interested in boys at all, and I didn't ever expect that you would date a farm boy; I mean, he's a little rednecky. As a 'popular and cool' kid, I always imagined that you would be with a preppy boy. Like a son of someone your dad works with, or the SCA president. I didn't see you going for a bear of a man."

"First...by whose standards am I 'popular'? And I would call him more a 'teddy bear of a man,' rather than a redneck. But honestly I'm as surprised as you. The last thing I was planning on doing is falling for a guy when I already have so much to worry about and plan. I don't have time to spend on a relationship, but when we're together, it's so natural and comfortable. He gets me in a way few people do."

"Well, I'm surprised, but I'm thrilled for you, as long as he makes you happy, as long as he doesn't break your heart — or I will have to kill him." Campbell throws her arm around Addison, holding her tightly, as if by holding her close she can make sure that the bond between them stays strong, regardless of boys, college or careers.

"What about Jamison? I noticed that the two of you are spending quite a bit of time together. Jamison is more the type who I expected to be with — maybe he's perfect for you?"

Campbell bursts out laughing, so much so that Addison looks around, embarrassed. She doesn't know why she is being laughed at; it isn't ridiculous to consider that Campbell might be interested in Jamison. He's cute, well dressed and they spend a lot of time together.

Catching her breath and calming down. Campbell waits until everyone has picked up their conversation again, and whispers, "You're kidding right?"

"No, I'm not, and I'm not sure why you would laugh so loudly. I mean, he's cute!"

"And *very* not interested in me."

"Why would you say that, Cams? You're adorable, smart, kind…"

"Because he's gay, Addison. You can't seriously tell me that you didn't know."

Her jaw drops and she feels stupid immediately. "I really had no idea, Cams. I'm so ignorant."

"Don't worry about it. He will be flattered that you thought he was cute enough to date *moi.*"

"Please, please don't tell him I didn't know. I'm humiliated."

"Okay, promise."

"Do his parents know? Do they support him?"

"Both his parents were pretty shocked when he came out. They were in pretty intense denial too. But his mom accepted it sooner than his dad and supports him now. I think she had to reset the way she views Jamison, and even though it's not easy, she tries really hard to be accepting. But his father has a really hard time with it. He and his conservative beliefs. He still considers it as morally wrong and doesn't quite believe him. He had been set on grandkids; I know it isn't what he had expected for his son's life. It isn't an easy life, especially in cookie-cutter McLean. His father is worried that their families will ostracize Jamison and that his grandparents will disown him, because they are catholic."

"Wow. My mind is blown."

"You won't treat him differently, will you? Lots of kids in that community suffer from depression and are at risk for suicide, so it's really important that as his friends we are there for him."

"I would never treat him differently. I wanted him to date you…now I need to find someone new who we can double date with. Is he dating?"

"Not now. In fact, I'm not sure he ever has, but I don't really know for sure, I try not to pry. It's a touchy subject since the guys he dates, or wants to date, may not be out yet."

"It must be really complicated for him."

"It is. When I asked him if it was hard to come out, he looked at me and said he has to come out every day, because every time he meets someone new, he has to reveal himself. That really struck me; I can't imagine how difficult that must be for him. I'm sure it's painful, but he has learned who his true friends are. Honestly, I think it's our parents' generation who struggle more with homosexuality than ours does. There are a few ignorant people who are haters, but I feel like most kids are surprisingly accepting of Jamison for sure, but also in general of gay kids at school. There will always be bullies who are narrow-minded and who are threatened by gay people, and in particular gay men."

"Wow, I had no idea. Thanks for trusting me."

In the natural flow of the conversation, Campbell turns to the girl sitting on her right, and Addison turns to her left and tries to catch what Mason and Jamison are talking about. It appears to be a much lighter conversation, namely the movie they plan on seeing. It is the newest movie adaption of a teen fad book series. Jamison is arguing that it is not art, while Mason says its purpose is to entertain, which it does. This is the second of a trilogy; Addison has read all the books, and is actually excited to see the movie.

Addison jumps into their conversation, "I don't care it's not art, I can't wait to find out how they create the vampire scenes. Will they actually show the bite, or will it only be implied?"

They go on to discuss the movie throughout the rest of dinner. As the bill arrives, everyone pulls out their credit cards to pay for their meals, and they head up to the movie. A few of the girls don't join them, because they have early swimming practice. Mason holds on to Addison's hand as they take the three escalators to the top floor where the movie theater is. They purchase their tickets, and thankfully, the eight o'clock showing isn't too crowded and they are able to get seats together.

As the movie theater goes dark, Addison is thankful to have Mason to herself. He wraps his arm around her shoulders, and she burrows into the nook of his shoulder and chest. She finds a space there which perfectly fits her head, and she settles in as the movie begins. Throughout, Mason has his arm around her shoulders while his other hand holds hers. She continually feels the electrical shocks run through her body. She can't believe that he has this effect on her. She wonders if couples who have been together for years still feel this way. As if Mason can read her mind, he leans over, grabs her chin with his hand, and gently places a kiss on her lips. She does not care that this relationship makes no sense, that they don't have a viable future together, she is thrilled to be with him, and she is going to enjoy every moment she can with him, until life takes them their separate ways.

10

Failure Makes Us Stronger

Friday, February 19

Addison spends the rest of the week studying four or five hours a night, after her taper track workouts. She only has time to check in with Mason after track and exchange short texts before she heads to bed. This week has been particularly difficult, completing her story for the magazine, putting her spread together, and editing others' stories plus managing her Trig homework, finishing her research paper and doing her Key Club duties; she is overwhelmed. It seems as if she has a quiz or test nearly every class, and the pressure is getting to her.

By Friday, Addison is a nervous wreck. Her appetite has been gone the last several days, she hasn't gotten enough sleep, and she is feeling sluggish and tired as she packs up her track gear. She has an early release today, which means she is missing class, which in turn equals more homework for the weekend. She wishes she could fast-forward to her freshman year in college and be wherever her destiny takes her. She is tired of worrying about every single assignment and performance, and how it might affect her future. It would be nice to live a little, like she did over the weekend.

She and Mason have plans to hang out after the track meet. She hasn't been so relieved for the weekend to arrive in a long time. She wants to sleep all day Saturday, but she also knows she has hours of homework again. Her APUSH assignment is going to take forever. Her classmates have said they have already spent five hours, counting only the reading and annotations. She plans on dedicating Saturday to working on that. Sunday to finishing her final edits and review of the magazine proofs so they can submit it to Mr. Peterson by Monday. She is a little disappointed in her fellow editors, who are likely in the same boat, but she has noticed that many of them have not touched their articles or spreads, so likely Sunday she will be texting and harassing her staff to finish their work so she can do hers.

By the time Mason and Addison get off the bus at the conference meet, Addison is a little calmer. She is worried though, because her legs are still a little stiff from Saturday's hike. They haven't felt as good as she had hoped. She begins to doubt why she went on the hike, and a small part of her resents Mason, because she knows she needs that record.

The day is warm and sunny. The air smells like spring, even though it is only late February. She can smell the small plants and worms starting to make their way to the surface of the soil. She loves spring, and she can't wait for the gardens to be in full bloom. Within a month, the early spring flowers will be up, and trees will be blooming. The downside of the warmer weather is that Addison knows she runs her best when it is brisk and cold.

When it is time for her run, Coach Turner pulls her aside, "Erhard, you got this. It's yours if you want it!

She smiles weakly, "I don't feel it Coach."

"Get your head in the game, kid. You need to visualize your run, step by step, turn by turn. Now go warm up and stretch."

She can see Mason off to the side, observing the conversation and her nervousness, and likely he is feeling a little guilty.

When Coach is done psyching Addison up, Mason walks over to her. He takes her face in his hands, the warmth of his rough hands enveloping her, "Addison, you can do this, it's okay. I have faith in you." He gives her a quick hug and peck on her cheek. Her stomach flips again. Now she doesn't know if it's him, or if she's just nervous.

As she gets ready for her start, she says a little prayer to Grandma, and hopes she can give her the extra strength she will need to not only win the conference, but to shave off another two-tenths of a second.

At the start of the race, she immediately knows what she has been sensing all day, that her legs are sluggish and slow. She tries to stay at the front, but she can't pass the second-place runner from Oakton High School. She tries to maintain her energy in order to stay competitive. She knows she's not going to make her time goal today, and now she is only concerned about cutting her losses and keeping her energy level enough to at least perform well on the relay.

As she crosses the finish line, she is deeply disappointed. She finishes in fourth place, her worst finish of the season. When Coach sees her, he shakes his head. "I knew your mind wasn't on this race, Addison. You have to pull yourself together. You know that nothing significant has happened since last week. You have simply psyched yourself out, worrying, and convincing yourself that you can't do this today."

"But, Coach, the hike over-tired me."

"Yes, and it was almost a week ago. Addison, the only damage that is happening is in your head. Shake it off and I want to see a killer race in the relay."

She walks off with a pit in her belly. She is sorely disappointed, not only in herself, but she has let Coach Turner and her team down. She is sure Tara is already over there persuading Coach that Addison shouldn't run anchor for the relay, and the worst part is, Tara is right this time.

Mason is there to meet her as she leaves the track. "Hey, Angel, how're you doin?"

She looks up at him, trying to avoid the tears she can feel well up in her eyes. "It pretty much sucked. Coach says it's all in my mind. But I didn't feel strong or powerful."

"I know, Angel, and I feel horrible because I shouldn't have taken you on that hike Saturday."

"Coach says it's not the hike, it's my head."

"Okay, let's be reasonable...did you lose your only chance to break the record?" He wraps his arms around her, holding her tight, his chin resting on the top of her head.

"No."

"Do you believe your running ability has irrevocably been

harmed?"

"No." She starts to smile, because she knows he is being reasonable, and he is letting her know that she hasn't lost it all.

"So, you will make it to regionals based on your time, right?" He moves her at arm's-length, so he can look straight into her eyes.

"Yes."

"Which means you have a week to get your head right, to rest your body, and to visualize your shattering of the record. Okay?"

"Okay." Mason pulls her into a giant bear hug and she finds her spot on his chest, the spot where she fits perfectly, the place where she feels completely safe and comfortable. She lets him hold her there until she has control over her emotions.

"Step-one, cool down. Let's cool down those legs and see if you can't convince them to pull it together for your relay."

"Okay…" Addison hates being weak, doesn't want to need Mason's motivation to pull herself out of her funk, but she is also pleased he's here with her, and he knows what to say to make her feel better.

After her cool-down, and watching Mason throw shot-put, she's ready for her relay. As expected, Tara has convinced Coach that Addison should not be anchor. Coach says he's giving her the first leg, in good faith that she has pulled her mind back together and can take the team to a strong start.

Addison does just that. It isn't her best run, and she can still feel a sluggishness in her legs as she sprints down the final 100, but she also knows it was far better than her individual run. She hands off the baton to Samantha, tied in first position with Yorktown. She watches as Samantha fights to stay in the top two, and then Marissa loses a little ground, sliding to third. When Tara takes the baton, she jettisons out of the starting area and immediately settles in behind the first-place runner, still from Yorktown. She cannot catch her, even in the last fifty meters, when clearly she is giving her last bit of energy. Tara crosses the finish line red-faced, out of breath, and angry.

"I can't believe I couldn't catch her. Addison, I wish you had been able to get a good lead for us to maintain. Yorktown's last leg was too fast for me to catch."

Samantha retorts more quickly than Addison can, "Maybe you

should've let Addison run the final leg then, Tara. Obviously you aren't able to run fast enough. I don't understand why you always pick on Addie."

"She can't even defend herself. So sad," sneers Tara.

Before Addison even has a chance to respond, defend herself, or challenge Tara, Tara stomps off.

"She thought this would be her moment of fame. She's so selfish on the track. I wish they would kick her off the relay, even though she is wicked fast," says Samantha.

"She needs to be a team player," Addison says. She doesn't want to worry about Tara or her selfish desire to be the star relay runner; she wants to find Mason.

With her disappointing track performance behind her, Mason and Addison decide to take advantage of the beautiful weather and grab a dinner-to-go and eat it in the garden at Addison's house. They drop Addison's car off at her house and run to Chipotle in McLean to grab some burritos. Despite the improved relay event, Addison can't shake her disappointment in today's races, and she realizes she really only has one more shot to break the record. With today's racing, she isn't guaranteed a spot at State.

It's after six by the time they have picked up their dinners. They sneak into the garden gate and follow the path towards the cottage, where they find a secluded bench. Mason can tell Addison is still upset. They settle in, and unpack their chicken burritos. They share the chips and salsa, Addison's favorite, and pull out their iced teas.

"I'm so sorry, I've been an unpleasant date tonight Mason."

"Ah ha, so it *is* a date. I was wondering if we were calling it dating yet."

"I'm really horrible, terrible actually, at playing games and being coy. I hope this is a date."

"Then there're two of us who aren't into toying with people's hearts. I wear my emotions pretty much on my sleeve. What you see is what you get. I can't promise you the world Addison, I can't give you your record, and I can't get you into Columbia, or make you famous. But, I can promise I will be honest with you Addie."

"That is a pretty serious promise. I really want all those other things, but I know I'm the only one who can get them for me. I won't ever expect someone else to do that for me."

"Angel, keep in mind that if you don't reach all those goals, those lofty and ambitious goals you have set for yourself, you will still be you. You will still be Addison, you will always be amazing, especially to me." Mason is turned towards her now, and his voice is low and gentle. What he says makes so much sense; hearing them from Mason, whom she admires, has more impact on her than if anyone else said it. For the first time in months the strain she has put on herself is lightened a little bit and she feels optimistic that things will work out for her.

"Thank you, Mason." She leans into him, and they look over her mother's garden, which is still dormant. She can sense the growth of the crocus and daffodils under the rich soil. She feels the promise of incredible beauty, as long as there isn't a frost that strikes while they are still tender sprouts.

11

Breaking Records and Dreams

Saturday, February 28

Addison ponders the heavily marked calendar on her desk. "Ten days between the conference meet and regionals," she says out loud to no one but herself. Mason's and Addison's relationship falls into a comfortable rhythm. Saturday has become the sun they orbit around. The week is too packed with Addison's class load, the school magazine, Key Club, and her focus on breaking the track record.

They make time for each other during the week by studying together, and Mason has taken up running to join Addison on her weekend runs. They are comfortable enough with each other that they can quietly sit in her kitchen studying and not talk, finding peace in the fact that at least they are in the same room. Often, Mason joins her mother and herself for dinner in the evenings. Addison wonders if his parents miss him, if they wish they had more time with him. He assures her that once spring comes, he will be spending all his weekends at the farm, and they will have enough of him.

This idea makes her sad. She is dreading spring for the first time in her life. She will miss their weekend dates and get-togethers with the group. Jamison, Campbell, William, Addison and Mason have spent several evenings together, hanging out at Rocco's, grabbing ice cream, or watching movies; most often at Addison's house. Addison's mom has always welcomed large groups of kids into her home. She keeps the basement kitchen stocked with snacks and drinks, and there is a library of blue rays they can choose from. Sometimes they play board games, which makes them all feel like the biggest nerds, but they laugh and compete late into the night. Addison can see that Jamison is quickly taking her place as Campbell's best friend, as Mason occupies Addison's free time.

The regional track meet is scheduled for March 1 at the Boo Williams Sportsplex in Hampton, Virginia. The meet will take place over two days. Both Addison and Mason will travel to the meet and will miss Tuesday and Wednesday of school. Addison feels torn, because missing school for two days means she will have missed seven classes and several quizzes, and it will be her job to make sure she gets all the work made up and quizzes taken before or after school. She wishes that these huge meets were held on the weekend, so she wouldn't have to miss so much classwork. On top of the nervousness she is feeling for breaking the record, she also feels anxiety of knowing she is missing critical work, as well as the final edits for the final draft of the magazine, her stomach is a tight ball of nerves, and she's having a hard time eating and sleeping.

As has become their routine, Mason talks her out of her anxiety attacks. Even in the middle of the night, she's texted him, assuming that he would see her text in the morning, and he's called her to help talk her back into a state of calmness. She is so grateful for his rock-solid attitude, his ability to help her feel grounded and reassess what really matters to her.

Despite the stress she's feeling about the track meet, she is looking forward to the bus ride with Mason, and knowing that he will be with her during the meet. Evenings will be filled with homework, pasta dinners and getting to bed early. She is rooming with her relay teammates, and she is nervous about how Tara will behave towards her. She sincerely wants to get along, so that both can be relaxed. She's considered requesting Coach keep her in the first leg of the relay, so that Tara will leave her alone. Only, she's pretty sure Coach will look at times alone and make a decision. His priority won't be keeping Addison and Tara from each other's throats. She is already dreading the outdoor track season and another battle for leadership on the relay.

"Hey, Angel, are you already packed and ready for the meet?" Mason and Addison are sitting in the sunroom, overlooking the left side of the garden; in the distance is Elizabeth's studio. Her mother has been in her studio all day, and her father has been at work, a typical Saturday at the Erhard's. It is a cold day, but the sun is bright and warm. They have been sitting in the sunroom for most of the day, studying, reading, and talking. Although most of the day she has spent working, it has been at a relaxing pace. Mason has been working on a paper for his AP Environmental Science class, and Addison has been making final edits to the magazine and working on a research project for her Russian class.

"Nah, not yet, I feel like if I get it all ready now, I will have to repack again on Monday, because I won't be sure that I have it all. Are you all set?"

"Yep, I'm all set. I'm a guy. It's not complicated for me. As long as I have my shoes and my wrist wrap. The rest is pretty unimportant, and my music of course."

"Oh... Do you have a special throwing mix...like 'Throwing Things' by Ned's Atomic Dustbin or 'One More Night' by Maroon 5 or 'Throwing Things' by Super Chunk? "

"You think you're a funny girl, don't you? I'm a deep and complicated man. You can't even guess what my music choice is. If you're really lucky I might let you listen to it on the ride down." His voice is serious, but his eyes are smiling at Addison. They have developed a teasing ritual which relieves the tension Addison feels. They go back to work with Mason muttering, "'Throwing Things', really has no clue."

After spending most of the day working on homework, Addison looks up at Mason, "What do you think about packing it up and heading to the Sculpture Garden in D.C. to go skating?"
"Huh. I haven't been skating in forever. I'll only consider it if you promise to not fall and break anything. I can't bear the guilt of another meet that I've ruined. "

"You know that was just in my head — I'm a dork. I psyched myself out. The good news is you're coming with me and you are my calming agent."

"Your own personal good luck charm." Mason says this, but Addison knows he blames himself for doubting herself at conferences. She knows he thinks he has taken her out of her normal routine. That he keeps her out late and has distracted Addison from her work and her focus. She doesn't know what to say to help him understand that it isn't his fault. That she thinks it's all worth it. Being with him makes her content.

"Let's not worry about regionals yet. I want to live a little, I want to enjoy my Saturday, and not spend the rest of the weekend wishing we had done something fun."

They swing by Mason's house on the way to D.C. His home is small and modest, and set in the part of McLean which was developed in the 50's. Most of the houses in his neighborhood are still the original ranch-style homes, with red brick, a large picture window set next to the front door, and two smaller windows on the other side of the front door. The style reminds Addison of advertisements she's seen from the 50's advertising new "individual homes" for young families. Only, the stark contrast between these small homes, and the renovated homes, which pepper each street, is drastic. Those newer renovated homes dwarf the classic homes. Yet, what they all have in common are the BMWs, Audis, Mercedes and Range Rovers parked in driveways. Despite being small and dated, homes in McLean are expensive. No home in McLean sells for less than $750,000, even the tiniest, most rundown house. Larger places are well into the millions. No question, small or not, no one who is short on money can afford to live in McLean.

Addison still has not met Mason's parents. She's nervous that they will be home today, and she isn't sure she is ready to meet them. It strikes her as strange that Mason has almost become the fourth member of her family, yet she hasn't even been introduced to his parents. She wonders if he is afraid that she will embarrass him, or worse yet, that he hasn't even told them about her. She knows that her mother and father would never let her spend this much time with a boy they hadn't even met. But then again, having a teen daughter is probably different than having a teen boy.

They pull into Mason's driveway, and he tells her he will be right back. His house is small, with the brick painted white, a winter wreath hangs on the front door. It's an attractive house, but knowing what his house in Marshall looks like, she can't imagine that his mother spends much time in this house. It suddenly occurs to her that perhaps only Mason lives here, maybe his parents only check in with him. How sad and lonely that would be. She doesn't know if she should ask him, or if she should wait for him to tell her. He certainly has talked about his parents with respect and love; she can't imagine that he actually feels abandoned.

As he is in the house, Addison thinks she sees someone glancing out of the window, and prepares herself for meeting his mom, finally.

When he comes out of the house, he locks the front door and tosses an old pair of skates in the back of his truck. He is wearing his jeans, a thick winter coat, a hat and gloves. He is ready for the weather to get colder as the day grows old.

"All set?" Addison asks, then gets the courage to ask, "Weren't your parents home today?"

"Nah, I'm gonna guess that Dad got called to the farm and Mom went to keep him company. She misses the farm when they're here. Even if it means driving back and forth two hours, she always jumps on the chance to go out there."

"Will they be back tonight?" Addison is surprised and wonders if it was Mason who looked out of the window, checking to make sure she hadn't driven off in his truck.

"Oh, I'm sure they will." Mason quickly changes the subject. "Bet you didn't know that I owned my own bona-fide pair of skates, did you?"

"No, I didn't. I'm not sure if I'm impressed, or scared."

"I used to skate a lot at the farm. There's a small pond about a mile in, between some of the fields, and my dad and I used to go out there on cold days and skate. Sometimes my neighbors would come over and we would play a pickup game of hockey. It wasn't anything fancy, but it sure was fun."

"I've skated often, but I've always rented skates. First I grew too fast to make my own pair worth it, and now I only go a few times a year, and it's easier to rent them."

"Have you skated at the Sculpture Gardens before?"

"My mom and I have always come around Christmas, if it's cold enough. It's absolutely beautiful, with Christmas lights strung in all the trees, the sculptures lit up and the National Archives in the background. It makes me think of Mom, the holidays and my childhood."

"I can't wait to see it. Do they have a place to warm my hiney?" Mason looks at her with an impish grin.

"They do; they have a cozy little restaurant where we can get the most decadent brownies and hot chocolate. It's even worth freezing your butt off for."

They make their way along Old Dominion Drive, onto Lee Highway, through Arlington, across the Theodore Roosevelt Bridge, and onto Washington D.C.'s Constitution Avenue. As they come down Constitution, they can see all the monuments' lights and despite the cold weather, people are everywhere, from sight-seeing tourists, to locals trying to get a run in. They pass the White House, which is always much smaller than she thinks it is going to be, even after having grown up seeing it.

They are lucky enough to find space along Constitution Ave, parking in front of the American History Museum, one of Addison's favorite museums. They park and use the ParkMobile app to pay for their parking and walk, hand-in-hand, towards the sculpture garden. The garden itself is blocked off with a large iron fence. Once inside, twenty-one modern sculptures made of bronze, cement, glass and aluminum scatter the grounds around the center piece, which is the skating rink. In the summer the rink is transformed into a beautiful fountain, where people can eat their lunches in the sun and wade their feet in the cool water. Looking at the frozen landscape today, it is difficult to imagine that in a few short months, the same garden will be smoldering in ninety-eight-degree weather, with one-hundred percent humidity. Washington, D.C. has to have one of the most divergent weather from winter to summer in the nation. Addison is happy it's cold today. It invigorates her. She and Mason line up to rent her skates and then sit on the benches along the rink to put them on.

They skate along the outside of the rink for the first several minutes, getting used to the icy surface, and the uncomfortable skates. As they skate along, Addison is impressed with the beauty of D.C. The park is surrounded by hanging white lights, and all the sculptures are lit with specialized lighting. Along the north side of the park stands the National Archives, with a huge banner advertising the latest exhibition, and lit up as if it is reflecting the moonlight. The ice rink is crowded, with young children learning how to skate, young couples like Addison and Mason holding hands and in their own world, and old couples holding each other up while slowly making their way along the wall. Addison looks at older couple, maybe in their sixties, and sees the history that they hold together by the way that they look at one another, and sense what the other needs. She wonders if she will ever find someone who makes her feel completely known and loved; could it be Mason?

"Ready for my tricks?" Addison looks into Mason's eyes as they slow down.

"Sure, show me what you can do."

Addison skates into the center of the rink, gaining speed as she does so. Her natural ability is evident with every glide of her skates. As she reaches the center, she spreads her legs wide, angling her toes in a little and starts to spin. She holds her arms like a ballerina would and brings her legs in closer as she spins; soon she is spinning so fast that her hair flies in a circle making an orbit around her head. She then brings her arms in and crosses them over her heart and continues to spin for a few moments before she sticks the tip of her skate into the ice to stop herself.

"I'm not gonna lie, I'm pretty impressed with you."

"Can you do any tricks? I love to do them, Cams and I used to spend hours together at the rink, pretending we were professional skaters when we were little."

"Other than keep my body vertical rather than horizontal? No."

"Wanna to see me jump?" She is feeling like a giddy little girl, excited to show off her tricks, invigorated by the cold, and inflamed by Mason's complete attention on only her.

"Sure, as long as you can promise me you won't pull a hamstring or something disastrous."

Addison is feeling fearless and reckless. She leaves Mason along the wall again and skates towards the center of the rink, again gaining speed. This times she goes further and makes a large circle to gain speed. He can see her getting ready for her jump, she bends her right leg at the knee and holds her other leg behind her and thrusts it forward, causing her to leave the ice and spin, landing on her left leg.

"Addison! That was too dangerous. Have you lost your mind? I think my heart may have stopped. Can you imagine if you got injured? Please, please, let's go get some hot chocolate and let your sanity return!"

They enter into the glass pavilion, which overlooks the garden and rink. The menu offers coffees, sandwiches, hot chocolates and all sorts of desserts. They each purchase a cup of chocolate and decide to choose a brownie to share. Once they have warmed up, Mason looks at Addison. "Seriously, I can't bear the idea of you being hurt on my watch. Can we please return your skates? We can walk around the mall if you aren't ready to go home yet, or we can go back to your house and watch a movie. Please don't put me in a place that I will feel guilty."

"Okay, let's walk the National Mall for a little while, and then head home and watch a movie."

They walk along the National Mall for about forty-five minutes, passing the National Gallery of Art, coming to the end of the mall in front of the Capital, and then walking along the opposite side of the mall and passing the Smithsonian Museums of Native American History, Air and Space, "The Castle" and coming back around at the Washington Monument. Then they walk back along the side of the Sculpture Gardens, returning past the American History and Natural History Museums. Addison loves D.C., she loves the arts, the history, the ability to see it all, the access that anyone and everyone has. It's a great symbol of the country. She especially loves it in the winter months when few tourists visit, and the majority of the people are inhabitants of the D.C. Metro area.

Once they return to the sculpture gardens, they walk back along Constitution Avenue to Mason's truck. She climbs in, and now she is cold and tired. She's looking forward to going home and cozily watching a movie, and trying not to worry too much about the upcoming meet. On their drive home the predicted light snow begins to fall.

On Monday, the worst possible thing happens to an athlete who is tapering so that she can peak at exactly the right moment. There is a huge blizzard. It is one of those storms which weather forecasters completely mispredict. A slushy sleet was supposed to fall starting in the evening, but temperatures drop much faster than anticipated, and the sleet falls, turning to ice on the pavement, and then quickly becoming a thick, heavy wet snow that leaves ten inches by morning; and adds another three inches during the morning hours. In typical Fairfax County Public School fashion, the school board makes the decision to close at 5:25 a.m., just as Addison finishes her shower and gets dressed.

She spends the day catching up on homework and reading. Mason comes over in his gigantic truck. He explains that this is exactly why he owns a Dodge Ram 2500, so that he can come see his girl rain, sleet, or snow; like a mailman. "I put those winter tires on for a reason, Addie. A snow like this out on the farm and you could have your truck stuck for a week without winter tread."

Addison receives the news she has been dreading via a GroupMe message from Coach: *Runners, unfortunately we cannot control the weather. Our Regional meet is delayed, and we are looking at next Thursday and Friday — March 10 and 11. I know this is going to throw many of you off in your tapering, but please remember to keep training. If you have a treadmill, use it. Winning isn't only a matter of physical fitness, it is a matter of your frame of mind as well. Each and every athlete in the region is in the same boat.*

Addison is devastated. She feels as if her chances at the record are slipping away with every day of snow and ice. Running indoors on a treadmill isn't the same as training outside.

She texts Mason, *did you get the text from Coach?*

Within moments Mason replies, *yes. im so sorry Angel. i know this throws a wrench in your tapering…the good news is…my truck can make it through the snow*

im so mad Mason. why did this have to happen?

things just happen babe. it sucks but like coach said, everyone is in the same boat.

can you come over? maybe everyone can come by to sled? you could get cams and Jamison

I can

The storm shuts down the system for most of the week. Roads are hardly cleared, and there is no chance that Addison can risk running on the roads, which already are narrow, and most don't have sidewalks. If she were to run outside, not only would she risk slipping and pulling a muscle, but being hit by a car is much more likely with snow encroaching on what little shoulder there is.

The production of the news magazine is slowed now too. Normally this week there would be a late night that all the editors spend at school with Mr. Peterson, editing and proofing the final magazine pages and sending them off to the printer. They are doing their best to hold an online meeting by texting, looking at pages and leaving comments for one another. By Wednesday morning, the magazine is ready to be sent to the publisher, but Addison isn't as comfortable with it as she would be if they had met in person. The cover of the magazine is a split photograph of Yale campus; a staff writer's parent took on a college visit; she had posed with a friend in lab coats. The other side is of Mason on his tractor at his parents' farm, a photo which he had on his phone from the fall harvesting season. The cover story headline is "Yale-bound or farm-tied: CBHS students follow their own dreams, or fall into their parents' footsteps." She hopes that students will see the article as a reminder to pursue their own dreams and what makes them happy, without insulting those who choose to conform to the education and career their parents have planned for them.

The snow is so wet and heavy that it isn't even fun to be outside. Wednesday afternoon Campbell and Jamison trudge through the snow to join Addison and Mason for some sledding. After twenty minutes in the snow, their pants are soaked through, and there is snow and ice in every crevice of their clothing. They quickly abandon the outdoors for dry clothing and a round of Carcassonne, a game of strategy and completely entertaining for the nerds at heart that they all are.

By Thursday she is caught up on all her homework and she is completely tired of being at home. The parking lots of the schools are finally clear on Thursday night, and students pull out of their snow-day delirium to grab their book bags and head back to the halls of Chain Bridge High. The roads are still too dangerous to run on, so their track practice is held inside, with the team running through the halls and up and down the stairs. It isn't ideal training, and Addison can feel her shins and joints with every step on the cement surface, but at least she is running with her team and gets to see Coach face-to-face.

Addison is relieved that by Saturday afternoon she can finally run outside again. By Monday, the team can practice outside. She hopes that now that it's March, there will be no more snow, no more delays, and her garden will start to show signs of spring again.

On Wednesday afternoon, the team meets outside of the school and loads into the charter bus and heads to Hampton, Virginia, for the regional meet. Mason and Addison share a seat again, and once again Mason tries to keep her calm and relaxed through self-deprecating jokes and talking about the upcoming edition of the magazine. The three-and-a-half-hour drive to Boo Williams Sportsplex goes by slowly, and Addison falls asleep on Mason's shoulder as he reads *The Great Gatsby* for his AP English class.

Addison settles into her hotel room at the Hampton Inn in Newport News, which she is sharing with Samantha, Tara and Monique. She and Samantha share one of the two queen beds, while Tara and Monique share the other. The entire team walks about three-and-a-quarter of a mile to the local Applebees, where they carbo-load and do some team bonding, but the underlying tone is both nervous and excited. Most of the athletes on this team had been hoping to peak the previous week, so that they could get a shot at going to states, or in some cases, they had hoped to be peak at states next week ready to break some records. The delay in the competition has them off their schedules, which can be frustrating, not to mention the less-than-ideal training weather from the last week.

On Thursday morning, Addison's parents join her at the Hampton for breakfast. She is nervous as she eats her habitual oatmeal and fruit; she stays away from coffee this morning, fearing that it will give her a sour stomach, or an accelerated heart rate. Her mother and father are here, and the fact that her father has taken the day off from the bank is nearly a miracle. He rarely takes time away, especially for a sporting event, but it is his way of showing Addison how much all this means to him and how proud he is of her.

Boo Williams Sports Complex is a 135,000 square foot indoor sporting event facility and is the largest sportsplex between Washington, D.C. and Greensboro, North Carolina. Its size is overwhelming, but it is also easy to disappear and find a quiet area to set up and stretch, without feeling the pressure of all the other athletes. CBHS is part of the 6A North Regional Meet, the most competitive division in the state.

As Addison is doing dynamic stretches after her mile warm up she feels a tightness in her left leg. She is lunging and stepping up, holding her knee near her chest. As her left leg comes up to her chest, she feels a twang and hears a pop. The pop is followed by a sudden excruciating pain on the back of her leg, near her glutes. She knows exactly what is happening, because she has seen it in other athletes. She falls to the ground, screaming in pain and frustration. She has torn her hamstring.

12

Perspective

Friday, March 11

The rest of the trip is a blur of doctor's visits and a drive back with her parents to McLean. She isn't even able to stay with Mason to watch him finish out his regional meet. After visiting her orthopedist, MRI and ultrasound, Addison has learned that she has a grade II tear in her hamstring. She can expect a several-month recovering, including physical therapy, and for the time being, complete immobilization and crutches. She is devastated. Her dream to break the state record as a junior is done. Not only will she not break the winter record, but she won't be fit enough for the spring track season, if she is even running by then. Now she has two more opportunities to break the record: in the fall in cross-county season, a totally different beast; or the following winter track season, a year away.

Addison is nearly inconsolable. She has spent most of Friday in her room with the lights out and curtains closed. Chandler has been her constant companion. Her mother has come in quietly to check on her and bring food she doesn't want to eat. Addison has been texting with Mason, but she hasn't picked up when he has called. She is too angry, disappointed and sad to speak to him on the phone, because in a moment, he will hear how devastated she is, and he will somehow find a way to blame himself.

Around nine in the evening on Friday, there is a gentle knock on her door. "Addie, may I come in?" It's Mason. He sounds almost afraid to enter her room. "Your mom said it would be okay to come by after we got back from the meet."

Addison sits up in her bed and quickly tries to straighten her tangled hair. She's still wearing the yoga pants and sweatshirt she wore to the doctor's. She has no make-up on, and her eyes are puffy from crying. "I'm not sure you want to see me this way, Mason."

"I always want to see you," he tentatively moves into her room...stumbling in the dark. "Mind if I turn on the light?"

"I got it." Addison reaches over and turns on her bedside lamp. Even that movement sends shooting pains up and down her leg. She groans as she straightens herself. Mason walks to her bedside quickly.

"Oh, Angel, I'm so sorry. I hate to see you in pain." He gathers her in his arms. "I don't even know what to say. I know you feel like it's the end of the world. I hope you know that it isn't."

"Don't even tell me I get another shot. I already know that I can't do spring track, and I'll be lucky if I'm back at the top of my game by the fall. By then, my applications will already be due. I don't know if I even have a shot at Columbia now." Self-pity consumes her and despite every effort to control herself, tears spill out of her eyes. "Oh I *hate* crying."

Taking her in his arms he whispers into her hair, "You know that isn't true, there are so many things you have going for you. Your stories alone can get you in. Honestly, I think the article that came out will be enough to get you some attention."

"Mason, I need a massive story, a story that is breaking, unveiling of some huge conspiracy. I need to force the school to change a policy, or better yet, the school board, if I'm going to get in on my writing alone. I need to uncover a huge mystery or secret. *That* will get me notoriety. Not a story about kids who choose not to become lawyers, but farmers. It's a good story, but it isn't an amazing story." Addison looks at Mason with anguish. She can't imagine where to find such a story, and a story like that brings its own tension and anxiety, and she doesn't know if she has it in her. Can she really take the risk an article like that would pose? Will her principal even allow a story that will reveal a secret, or demand a change in the school system? "I don't know where to find a story like that, Mason. I feel dead inside. Not to mention that I will go crazy without running to relieve the stress and anxiety in my life. How will I survive with no running for months to come?"

Mason wraps her in his arms. There is nothing he can do or say, and Addison knows it. She needs him to hold her and wishes he was able to make her hurt go away, or find her a story, or make her get into Columbia. But she knows he can't do any of those things for her. Only she can control her future, only she can find her own destiny, and Mason can sit by and hope it includes him in some way.

Finally, around midnight, well after his curfew, and well after her parents have gone to bed, Mason, who has been sitting on Addison's bed cradling her, still in her yoga pants and sweatshirt, extracts himself from her sleeping arms, and sneaks out of her room.

Saturday morning, Addison is awoken with a start. Her mother is shaking her awake. She is confused. It's Saturday, she is in pain. She remembers her leg; she remembers that Mason was lying next to her when she fell asleep. She isn't sure why her mom is frantic. Was she worried about Mason being there, has something happened?

"Honey, wake up. Are you up?"

"Mom," Addison rubs her eyes, she has been in a deep sleep, probably brought on by her painkillers and her emotional exhaustion. "What's going on? Did something happen?"

"Campbell has been calling since seven this morning. She's hysterical. I couldn't understand a word of what she said. Can you please call her? I'm scared something has happened to someone. Maybe one of her sisters?" Campbell and her family have been close friends of Addison and the Erhards for years. Even though she isn't nearly as close to Campbell's sisters, they are still an important part of all of their lives, and the idea that something may have happened to one of them is terrifying.

"Okay, Mom. Where is my phone?" Addison is having a hard time clearing her mind. "When did Mason leave?" Elizabeth reaches for Addison's phone, which is charging on the nightstand.

"I feel like a horrible mom. You were so upset, and he seemed to have broken through your armor yesterday, so I checked on you at eleven and you were sitting and talking calmly, so I went to bed. I left him with you. I should never have done that. But your dad and I were so exhausted from the last few days, and you are almost eighteen. You don't need your mommy to make it all better now; I understand that in some ways, you need Mason more than me. If you would have asked me a year ago, I would never have allowed him to stay with you unsupervised, but you are so responsible. I let it go."

"It's not like anything can happen with a torn hamstring and a leg in a splint." Now Addison is annoyed. She doesn't need her mom to even imply that anything would happen. She isn't ready to discuss it, or think about it at the moment. "Can I have my phone, please?"

She sees that she has several texts from Campbell. *Addison. Text me. Now.* Another: *Addison: wake up and call me ASAP.* There are also five missed calls. Now Addison is getting really worried. She clicks on Campbell's number. Campbell picks up after the first ring. Immediately it is obvious that Campbell is upset. She is sobbing, she is trying to catch her breath in hiccupy jerks. "Addie... Addie."

"What is it, Cams? You're scaring me!"

"It's Jamison." Another gasp and hiccup. "He was, was, was h-h-h-hit." Again, Campbell loses her ability to communicate. She takes a moment to take a breath. "It w-w-w-was a hit-and-run. He's in a c-c-c-oma at G-g-g-georgetown Hospital."

"No, nonononononono. It can't be. Oh God! No!" The image of Jamison lying on the side of the road, unconscious as a car speeds away assaults Addison's imagination. What kind of person would hit someone and keep going, without a thought of what damage they have done? "When did this happen? Who found him? Is he going to be okay?" A million questions run through Addison's mind, she can't get the out fast enough.

Campbell takes a few moments to collect herself. Addison nearly dies of anticipation. Finally, Campbell is able to get the entire story out. "They found him around 5:20 this morning. He was running along Georgetown Pike, on the side of the road because the sidewalk was still icy. It was around the bend near Colonial Farm Road. The police said they think the driver never saw him. Maybe they thought they hit a deer, maybe the driver was still drunk from a late party on Friday. Thank goodness another man was running and spotted him. It must've been within ten minutes, and Jamison was breathing, but unconscious. He hit his head badly. There's a brain bleed they are trying to stop. His lung is collapsed, he has a broken right leg, arm and shoulder blade...," another long pause, and a deep breath, "They don't know if he will wake up. Oh Addison, it is so horrible. I can't imagine a life without Jamison in it."

"I don't understand Cams. I don't get it."

"Addie, can you come over here?"

"You know I would, but my leg is in a splint, I can't go anywhere yet; I'm bedridden at least for the weekend."

"Okay, then I'll come to you. I need a friend. I need you Addie."

"I'm so sorry, Cams. Want my mom to come get you so you aren't driving upset?" As she says this, she looks at her mother, whose hand is over her mouth, and her eyes wide. She is nodding 'yes'.

"Okay, that would be nice, Addie."

"She's on her way."

While her mother is out getting Campbell, Addison gets herself out of bed and maneuvers her way down the stairs. With this dose of reality putting things in perspective, daily problems seem suddenly minor. Yesterday she couldn't get out of bed because of an injury and the loss of a record. Today she would trade anything to see Jamison wake up. Now getting up and coming downstairs on crutches seems like a tiny hill to conquer, while finding a way to bring Jamison back is the mountain she must scale. If she only knew how to do it.

Addison, Campbell and her mother sit in the family room, drinking tea and coffee and keeping each other company. Right away Addison's journalist's mind jumps to its job, which is to uncover what has happened. "It isn't possible for the driver to disappear into thin air. There has to be some sort of evidence he or she left behind."

"Well, being the non-investigator that I am, the only resource I have are my crime shows." Campbell says dryly, with a hint of humor in her voice. Her dark brown eyes are red rimmed, and her fair complexion is tear stained. Her dark blond hair is haphazardly tied into a ponytail. "Those investigators would get pictures of the tire tracks and samples of the dirt. They would also be looking for something that might have fallen off the truck."

"Do you think they have it roped off?"

"When we were driving by on our way here, they were cleaning up their investigation. I bet they're gone now," says her mother helpfully.

"Mom, would you be willing to drive Campbell over there and see if we can get some pictures of what's left of the crime scene?"

"Sure, I'm not sure what will still be left, but I'm willing to try."

When they return, Mrs. Erhard and Campbell have photos of the entire area.

"I'm not sure how much of this is meaningful; it will be really hard to know which tracks belong to the car that hit Jamison, but we took as many as we could. It's a dangerous turn, and we were worried about being hit too. There were several tracks slightly onto the shoulder. It was pretty cold earlier this morning, but now that the sun is out the tracks are softening a little. The spot where Jamison was lying is obvious, and you can see the tracks running onto the side of the road. There are two sets of tracks that seemed likely to be associated, there are deep thick tire tracks, and then there are smaller, much thinner tracks. You can also see where the ambulance backed up to load Jamison. Between all the footprints and tracks, and the wet mud, it is really hard to make sense of it."

"I wonder if the police station had any more luck, and how we could get access to what they know." Addison's mother is thinking out loud, but she is saying what Addison has been considering.

"I wonder if I can use my press credentials to get some of their evidence," says Addison. "It might be a stretch, but since Jamison is a student at our school, I could argue that as a school reporter I want to find more information about the mystery."

"Let's call on Monday. I bet they are inundated today, and it's possible they already know who it might be," says her mother reasonably.

Addison suddenly realizes that Mason doesn't know. She hasn't talked to him since she heard. "I'm going to call Mason. I'm sure he hasn't heard." She calls and gets his voicemail, which makes sense since they are in the fields today, getting ready for the planting season. She leaves him a message asking to call as soon as he can. She also sends him a text, in case he doesn't have time to listen to the message.

Later that afternoon, Mason finally calls Addison back. "Hey, Angel, I saw that you called me. Everything okay? You didn't sound right."

"I've got some bad news, Mason. Jamison has been hit by a car. It happened early this morning. He's in a coma." Addison has to say all of this in one breath in order to get it out without breaking down.

"Oh, God. No!" There is a long pause on the line. Addison can hear him trying to control his emotions and his breathing. "Where did it happen? Who hit him? How does something like that even happen?"

"He was running on Georgetown Pike, and he was coming around the turn; we think the car was headed towards Great Falls. It clipped him on his right side. His arm and collarbone are broken and he hit his head pretty badly. It was a hit and run. The driver didn't even stop! Mason, how does someone do that? I can't imagine there are people like that on this earth."

"Addie, we have to find who did this. We have to do it for Jamison."

13

Uncovering Clues

Monday, March 14

On Monday, Addison is able to get up and dressed for school. Mason comes to pick her up since she can't drive with her leg in a brace. He comes up the porch steps; despite all the sadness of the last five days, his face brightens as soon as he sees Addison. He helps her into the car. "Is it my imagination or is your truck lower?" She is grateful that it seems lower, as it has always been a struggle to climb into the truck, and with her crutches and leg, she has been worried she wouldn't get in without a massive and embarrassing struggle.

"Very good. Yes, I took off the winter tires. I wanted the truck to be a bit lower for you, and besides now that it is spring planting season and I'll be traveling out to the farm more, it saves a ton on gas, and I'm pretty positive we won't be getting anymore big snow storms now that it's March. It should save you about four inches in getting up and down from the truck."

"Your timing is impeccable." She feels such a close connection with Mason. He is so thoughtful and caring. Perhaps she loves him, although she's not ready to say it yet.

When they get to school, Mason carries her bags in for her,

they head down the hall towards the journalism room. Addison wants to find out if Mr. Peterson thinks that she can get access to police evidence as a school reporter. As they walk through the halls, they can hear the undercurrent of conversation about Jamison's accident. Those who are friends with him are obviously upset, but it surprises Addison that those kids who haven't taken the time to get know Jamison, or who don't go in the same circles, seem upset too. She wonders if it is because he is someone they could have known, someone whom they passed in the halls, or someone they sat next to in class or lunch and that gives them a connection. Or is their distress a more human reaction, the fact that this could happen to anyone of them, that they acknowledge that regardless of who Jamison is or could become, his life is precious too? For many kids walking the halls, he is the first of their generation who has faced the fact that teens' lives are fragile too. So many young people live under the illusion that they are indestructible, that their success and happiness is a guarantee simply by the fact they are young. When one of their own is threatened, and their life hangs in the balance, it is a shocking awakening from the innocence of youth.

Addison gets to the newsroom, and Mr. Peterson is thankfully at his desk checking his emails. "Mr. Peterson, how are you?"

"I'm o.k. Addison. How about you? I know you are pretty good friends with Jamison."

"Actually, that is exactly why I wanted to come see you this morning. Do you think I could speak to the police department using my news magazine credentials? I want to write an investigative story about Jamison's accident. I wanted to see if they would let me look at some of the evidence. Would they allow that?"

"Legally, they have no obligation to show you any evidence. They can keep all evidence secret until there is a trial. For obvious reasons, they may not want to share this information. For example, if you see something truly incriminating in the evidence, you could warn the culprit, so they would keep it secret. Now, that being said, often with hit-and-run accidents, the police go to the media, asking for help, requesting anyone who may have seen the crime, or suspicious cars in the area, to come forward, as the local news stations have been showing the last few days. Perhaps if you approach the police and offer insider information, for example, you know many people in the community because you live nearby, or that you could help get information to the community through social media, you may gain some access. But of course, ethically, you would really need to help push out that information so that the culprit can be caught."

"That's exactly my goal, to find who has done this, and to expose him or her. I want to find who did this to Jamison, and I want them punished."

Addison is satisfied that she can convince the police to share some of their information with her if she can help them find the culprit. She struggles to gather up her bags and she and Mason head back into the hallway. As she is about to leave, Mr. Peterson calls after her, "Be careful, Addison, these investigations can be messy and dangerous."

That afternoon, Mason drives Addison to the local police station. Neither Addison nor Mason have track practice any longer, as Addison is injured and Mason did not qualify for the state competition. As they drive down Dolly Madison Boulevard, Addison is struck again with the strangeness that a few days can make. Before Jamison's accident, just days ago, she had been self-centered and egotistical, worrying only of her own broken dreams; today she is relieved to be free of track practice so she can go about something far more important: finding out what happened to Jamison and who is responsible for his accident.

They pull into the police station and walk up to the front desk. "May I help you?" asks a polite, heavy-set and middle-aged female police officer at the front desk. "Yes, my name is Addison Erhard, I'm a reporter with *Inside Chain Bridge News Magazine*; this is Mason Gentry, who is assisting me today." She glances at Mason, whose lips tighten, and she realizes she should have checked with him what his role was going to be...perhaps being an "assistant" is a little presumptuous. "We are wondering if we could speak with the investigator who is handling the Jamison Randolph hit-and-run case."

The officer's face turns stern. She is no longer friendly or welcoming. "I'm not sure that the officer in charge is speaking with the media."

"Could you please check for me? As you can see, it has taken a bit for me to come all the way in on my crutches, I've recently had an accident. It would be really nice if you could ask for us." Addison shamelessly uses any method she can to get her information. Let the officer believe it is an "accident," implying car, and let the officer take pity on her. She will do what it takes, even if it takes a bit of manipulation.

"I'll try. Please have a seat." She sighs heavily as if this task will be a burden for her.

Addison and Mason sit in two chairs close to the desk, where they can overhear the officers' conversations. In a quiet, but not inaudible voice, she makes a phone call. "Officer Rodriguez? Hi, this is Officer Spears. I have a young lady and gentleman here from the *Inside Chain Bridge News Magazine* who would like to speak to you about the Randolph accident...Yes, sir, they are quite young...I'm not sure...she is on crutches, sir, says she's had an accident...not sure, sir. All right." The officer replaces the receiver in its cradle. "Young lady, young man? Officer Rodriguez is willing to speak to you if you can wait about thirty minutes."

"Yes, ma'am. We can certainly wait." She turns to Mason and whispers, "I think they are testing our seriousness by making us wait."

In the interim, Addison brainstorms what she is going to ask. She wants to present herself as an asset to the officer, so that he is willing to share information with her, without making it seem as if she is going to exploit him, or the information he gives her. When Officer Rodriguez finally comes to get them, it has been closer to forty-five minutes.

Officer Rodriguez is a large man, but not as large as Mason. He has dark hair and a tan complexion and defies the stereotype of an officer who eats donuts and sits in coffee shops. He clearly takes good care of his health, because he is in great shape. He wears small dark-framed glasses, and his hair is neatly trimmed, not quite a military cut, yet a bit more stylish, without being trendy. Addison guesses that he must be in his mid-to-late thirties. "I'm so sorry to keep you both waiting so long, I had several things that needed to be finished before I could see you. Please follow me." He takes them through the double doors, into a portion of the station which is lined with officers' desks. It is now about four in the afternoon and many of the desks are already empty; a few officers are on the phone making calls, while others are talking in groups of two and three. Addison has to maneuver her crutches between desks and past office equipment to the end of the room where there are small offices with windows looking out into the larger room. The officer gestures for them to sit with their backs towards the window, and he sits facing them. It isn't quite an interrogation room, but it isn't a comfortable or welcoming room either.

"How can I help you two?"

"We are student journalists from Chain Bridge High School. We are aware that there was a hit-and-run accident early Saturday morning involving a student from our school. We also gathered that your press releases over the weekend have garnered little help in terms of finding the driver of the car which hit Jamison. We would like to offer our help."

Officer Rodriguez gives them a skeptical look and gazes over the two of them, Addison with her leg in a splint, and their obvious young age. "May I ask how you think you could help us?" He is trying to be serious, the corners of his mouth curve upwards, and his eyes twinkle. Addison assumes he thinks they are kids playing grown-up, and she is infuriated.

"Officer, Rodriguez, was it?"

"Yes."

"Well, sir, first, I live over a little over half mile from the accident site. My research says that local residents are often the best sources for leads because they know the neighborhood and its patterns. It's possible that a neighbor of mine may have seen something suspicious, but aren't making the connection. If I know a little more about what type of vehicle it was, I may be able to pinpoint some leads. Also, kids love nothing more than gossip on social media. Twitter and Instagram blew up within hours of Jamison's accident. These kids are dying to find some way to help Jamison. We can help direct the comments if we know a little more of what happened that morning. There might be someone who knows someone who was out on the road at the same time or in the same area. Any of those could be leads. Mason and I can troll the feeds to see if anything comes up."

The officer looks at them silently. Addison can see that he is more seriously contemplating her suggestions. He is taken off guard by her well thought-out ideas and explanations. She holds Mason's hand under the desk. He looks as nervous as she is feeling. If the officer has faith in them and shares some information, maybe there is some chance of finding out who hit Jamison.

"Well, I must say that I'm impressed. You seem to have done some research already. I'm not as active on social media as you are, and although I do know that we, as a station, use social media to push out press releases, I hadn't thought of using it in the same way that you propose. However, I want to be perfectly upfront and clear with you on two things. Firstly, you are to use any information we share with you only for the pursuit of justice in this case. If you use the information you find to harbor a criminal or hide further evidence, you will be charged with aiding and abetting a criminal. That is a serious crime with no witnesses. Secondly, you must understand that almost always, hit-and-run accidents remain unsolved. Especially in a case like this, where the runner was alone on the street, and there appear not to have been any other vehicles on the road. Finally, the area in which Jamison was lying is a high traffic area. By the time police officers got there, there were already many tire treads and disturbances made to the area. Jamison was lying deep in the ditch, and many cars had driven past him during the ten or twenty minutes that he lay there. It is also a deeply wooded area, and although we have done a sweep of the area, there may be evidence hidden in the leaves, in the snow or mud that we were unable to find, and may never find. Just because we share what little evidence there is with you does not mean that you or I will be any closer to discovering who hit Jamison. The best hope is that he wakes up and is able to identify the car and or driver who hit him. Frankly, with the type of brain injury that he has, he is highly unlikely to remember anything at all, *if* he wakes up at all. It may be months or years, and by then, the vehicle and its owner will be long gone."

Addison is visibly disappointed. She had truly and whole-heartedly, and naïvely, believed that she would walk in, find some critical evidence and make a connection that only she and Mason could make, and solve the mystery. She also is convinced that Jamison will wake up soon, and will be as he was when she saw him on Wednesday after school. "Officer, I'm not going to lie. I'm disappointed to hear all this, but I believe that Mason and I can help. Will you share your evidence with us?"

"Yes, but I'm afraid we don't have much. There are photos of tire tracks, and a photo of where Jamison lay, and a guess of where he was hit, but as of now, we can only guess two items: either the car was driving fast, or it was a large car or truck. There are two dominant tracks, that of a large vehicle with thick tires, and that of a much smaller and lighter tire track. Both drove on the shoulder the morning of the accident, we know this because they were rather fresh, and based on how much they had melted and how much mud was displaced, we estimate they were made near the same time. However, we cannot locate any further evidence. We checked the area for debris, but we found nothing. Either all of it has been buried in the mud, or there was none." Officer Rodriguez opens his laptop and keys in a few items. He turns the laptop around and shows Addison and Mason the photos of the tire tracks and the location of Jamison's body, and where they believe he was when he was hit, and how far his body traveled, based on his injuries.

After leaving the police station, Addison and Mason decide to visit Jamison before visiting hours are over, and before they head home to do homework. Addison is certain that if she sees Jamison, her desire to find the driver of the car will be even stronger. Addison texts Campbell: *Mason is gonna take me to see Jamison. we just got done with the police can you meet us there.* Within a moment, Campbell responds: *im already here. His mom had to take a break, promised I would stay with him until she got back.*

When Mason and Addison arrive at the hospital, they find that Jamison's parents have added them onto the approved visitor list. The nurse explains that this means they will be treated similarly to family and that the doctor and Jamison's parents agree that their presence could help in Jamison's recovery and his chances of coming out of the coma.

As they walk into Jamison's room, they are shocked by the sight that greets them. Jamison is the intensive care unit, and he is connected to machines, with a mask covering his mouth, pumping air into his inert lungs, his left leg is in a harness and a cast. The right arm is in a cast from his shoulder to his hand and is strapped to his chest. His head is bandaged where the surgeons have operated to relieve pressure from his brain. He has scrapes and bruises over the skin that isn't covered in gauze. Addison isn't sure she would know it was him if Campbell hadn't been sitting next to him.

Campbell is sitting at Jamison's side. She looks tired, her eyes are still red rimmed from crying and lack of sleep. She is holding Jamison's right hand and is talking to him when Addison and Mason enter the room.

"Hey, Cams. How are you holding up?"

"I'm so scared for him. The doctors said that we should talk to him, that hearing his friends and family may help him pull out of the coma. They think that talking helps bring the brain functions back. I don't know, but I feel better when I talk to him, makes me miss him a little less."

Addison and Mason pull chairs next to Campbell and sit with her. They talk about school that day, trying to keep things light. Addison is burning to tell Campbell what they learned at the police station, but she is worried that if she talks about it with Jamison laying there, that it will somehow bother him. They talk as if they are sitting in Addison's basement, pretending that Jamison is napping. It feels forced, and it's uncomfortable, but it is also reassuring that they are with him, and that he is still with them. Addison and Mason stay with Campbell for an hour, and then Mrs. Randolph returns, and other family members start trickling in. Mason, Addison and Campbell leave together and head to the cafe in the lower level to talk about the police reports.

After showing Campbell all the photos and retelling the interview with Officer Rodriguez, they discuss what they know. There were two cars that went off the road and into the muddy shoulder roughly around the same time. They presume that one of the tracks is the driver who hit Jamison, and that the other one may have slowed down in an attempt to see something along the side of the road, presumably Jamison. The question is, which car is the one who hit Jamison? There is no evidence in the forest, there is nothing on Jamison that would betray what kind of car it might have been. The two sets of tire tracks suggest one light and small car, and the other tacks are from much bigger vehicle, probably an SUV. It's not a lot to go on. The next question is who would be driving on Georgetown Pike at five in the morning, and why the heck was Jamison out running that early on a Saturday, and why was he running on the road? Anyone who has driven down Georgetown Pike knows that running on the road is dangerous, especially at night. Addison feels angry towards Jamison for taking such a risk. But then she thinks back on her own decisions and the mistakes she's made. Life is such a gamble, and every day people take risks, and it's either luck or destiny that determine who is going to survive.

Leaving the cafe feeling as frustrated and hopeless as before, Mason and Addison head back to her house to eat dinner and do homework. The drive back to McLean is quiet, both she and Mason are thinking of all the possibilities and how they can solve the mystery of Jamison's accident. The fact that most hit and runs are never solved does not bode well for their quest, and both Addison and Mason feel depressed and frustrated by this fact.

14

Following Trails

Tuesday, March 15

On the Tuesday following the accident, Addison and Mason decide to start Facebook and Twitter accounts to see if anyone saw anything, or knows anything. Maybe a neighbor's car is damaged, or they heard something or someone discussing the accident. It's more likely that someone would post this to social media than to bring it up to the police. While Addison is creating the accounts titled "Justice for Jamison Randolph," Mason is scouring Twitter, Facebook, Instagram and Snapchat to see if he can find any references to Jamison and what might have happened. There are many posts about keeping Jamison in prayers, finding the driver, etc., but little substantial information that they can use to find the driver.

As soon as the page is up, they start to share it with everyone on their friends lists, and with all their followers. Within an hour they have over five-hundred followers on the Twitter account. Information starts coming in. Most of it is not new information, but they are hopeful that something will give them a lead.

By the evening, there is a post on the Twitter account from @m4ttdr4tt: *Dude, my neighbor's jaguar has this massive dent on the bumper #savejamison.* Another comes in twenty minutes later from @sammitch: *My neighbor leaves every morning at five to head to the gym. Even Saturdays #savejamison.* The leads keep coming in. Now Addison and Mason have to find a way to use the information to track down who was driving down Georgetown Pike that morning, and who might have hit Jamison.

They message @m4ttdr4tt and @sammitch privately and ask for the address for the Jaguar and the five-in-the-morning gym rat. They plan on knocking on the door and asking questions on behalf of the school magazine. They suspect that if the driver is guilty, there will be anger and refusal to talk. If the driver is innocent, they won't mind an interview from the school news magazine. Over the next twenty-four hours there are more leads than they can handle. They decide to follow some of the bigger leads, especially the ones they think they can handle as news reporters from the school and share the rest with Officer Rodriquez.

Wednesday after school they head out for their first set of interviews. First to the Anderson home, whose neighbor spotted a banged up bumper and relayed that information via Twitter. Addison is still on her crutches, so Mason has to help her. The ground is still soft and muddy as the last of the snow melts, and making her way out of the truck and up the drive and front steps is still a challenge. Addison hopes that by Friday when she sees the doctor again, she can get off her crutches.

They pull up to a house off Sorrel Street, a large home with a circular drive in front. The Anderson's house and yard are not as large as Addison's, but it is an impressive home by anyone's standards. Mason puts the truck into park and walks around to help Addison out. Addison is once more grateful that Mason had the insight to put his summer tires on. She knows he used the excuse of the end of winter, but she also understands that he did it to be helpful to her. As he holds her arm with his big and steady hand, she is consumed with a warm feeling that starts in the pit of her stomach and radiates throughout her body. She knows that what she is feeling is love. She couldn't imagine a better partner to help her through this difficult time.

They approach the front door, with Addison awkwardly making it up the steps. She hopes that someone is home who will answer the door and make all this worth it. They ring the bell, and through the door she can hear footsteps racing across the wooden floors, skidding to a stop as a child's voice yells, "I got it, Mom!" Addison is filled with a feeling of relief knowing that someone is home and perhaps they will get an answer.

"Hi," a young boy of seven or eight answers the door. His blond hair covers the top of his face, with bright blue eyes peeking through the thin strands. He is dressed in basketball clothes, and Addison assumes that he is either coming from practice or about to head out.

"Hi, I'm Addison from Chain Bridge High. Is your mother or ..." Without waiting for the rest of her sentence, the boy turns from her and yells at the top of his lungs, "MOM! It's someone from the high school selling stuff!"

"Actually, I'm not selling anything ..." but the boy has already run to the back of the house. Addison can hear the mother's footsteps coming down the stairs. The door is still open, and it feels awkward without a person guarding the entrance.

"Samuel?! Where did you go? You can't leave the house wide open!" An exasperated woman comes into the open doorway, brushing her hair from her eyes. She is small, stunning and dressed in a smart and expensive Burberry outfit and sleek pointed boots under her checked slacks. "I'm sorry, what are you selling? We aren't really in the market unless it's Girl Scout Cookies, of course." The mother has a friendly and open demeanor, and despite her beautiful clothing, seems a little distracted and overwhelmed.

"Hi, Mrs. Anderson, I'm Addison Erhard, and this is Mason Gentry. Actually, we aren't selling anything, that was a miscommunication. We are from CBHS's news magazine."

"Oh. Okay. How can I help you?"

"We were wondering if we could interview you. We are doing a story on the hit-and-run involving Jamison Randolph, a CBHS student."

"Um, sure, not exactly certain how I can help." Now she is fidgety and a little exasperated. She turns her left wrist over and looks at her watch. "I don't have long; I need to have Samuel to basketball in twenty minutes."

"It will be a few moments. We are getting community perspective on the accident. Are you aware that one of our students was hit early Saturday, down the road, on Georgetown Pike?"

"Yes, I did hear that. People here are pretty upset because it was down the road. I hear he is a nice boy."

"Yes, it has affected our school deeply. The student body is devastated, especially because there are no answers in terms of who hit him. Do you believe that the road is safe? Should someone have cleaned the sidewalk to avoid the need to run on the road?"

"That turn always scares me. I really don't understand why the boy was running on the road that morning. It seems like a bad idea to me, especially at that turn, and scary. I absolutely think that the city should be held accountable for not clearing the sidewalks."

"Do you have ideas of who might have hit him?"

"Wouldn't that be a question for the police?" Addison can tell that she is already irritating Mrs. Anderson.

"Well, you know how people talk and find out what's going on in neighborhoods. We figure it is probably someone who lives nearby. Have you seen any suspiciously damaged cars?" Addison is looking for guilt or fear, or defensive behavior in Mrs. Anderson, an indication of possible guilt.

"This does not feel like an interview about my perspective on the accident. I don't like the direction this is taking." She's now clearly irritated. Addison imagines her Jaguar sitting in the garage with the dented bumper. "I'm not going to report a neighbor when I have no knowledge of anything."

"Mrs. Anderson," Mason interjects, "we by no means were trying to put you on the spot. We were wondering if you noticed anything suspicious."

"No. No, I did not. I wish you luck, but I really need to go now." Before she is even finished speaking, she closes the enormous front door with a thump.

"What do you think?" Mason asks her as they head back down Georgetown Pike. His eyes are focused on the road. He seems serious and agitated. Addison wonders if he hates confrontations, or if he is worried about Jamison, or is it the helpless feeling she has trying to figure out what has happened to Jamison.

"She was certainly not comfortable with us being there. I think she was trying to put on the air that she was helpful, but I don't think she wanted to talk about any of it."

"Do you think that her car could have been the one that hit Jamison?"

"I have an idea. She is leaving for basketball. Let's sit out near the end of the street and see if she is driving the Jag. If she is, then she isn't nervous about being seen with a damaged car. If she's driving another car, then I would guess that she doesn't want to be seen in a car with evidence."

"Or, she could drive one of her other cars because it's more convenient."

"Let's see, okay?"

Mason turns the truck around and heads back to Mackall Farms Lane, where they park their car. It is kitty-corner from Sorrell Street. It's a little hard to hide a huge truck, but there are many trees and bushes that will mask it to the unsuspecting eye. After about ten minutes of waiting, they see a large Cadillac SUV pull out, and Mrs. Anderson is driving. Not only that, but she keeps scanning the roads and driveways, well after the traffic has cleared. Eventually, her eyes fall upon their truck, and she has direct eye contact with Addison. Mrs. Anderson's Escalade tears out of the street and flies down the road towards Churchill Elementary, presumably where basketball practice is held. They can see her face as she passes them; it is stern and artificially focused on the road ahead of her. She does not look happy.

"Well, that isn't exactly incriminating, but it sure makes her seem suspicious, don't you think, Mason?"

"I don't think she has confessed yet, and in this country you *are* innocent until proven guilty, remember, Addison? Let's think about what we know." As he talks, he pulls out onto Georgetown Pike again, heading for their next interview. "She was friendly initially, but became more agitated while we spoke about damaged cars and neighbors knowing."

"Yes, and although you could argue that teenagers at the door are irritating, she didn't become irritated until we started to dig a little deeper about the accident."

"We also know that she drives a Jaguar, but that we could not see it at the house, and that she chose another car for today. "

"Mason, do you think we could peek in the garage and see if her Jaguar is there? Maybe we can see if there's damage?"

Without hesitating, Mason turns the truck around for the second time. "I sure hope Mr. Anderson isn't hanging out in his garage when we pull up."

"This is McLean; he will be at work until eight or nine. I'm sure it's fine. If he's there, we will say we lost a key and came back looking for it."

"You are surprisingly fast at coming up with little white lies, Addison. Should I be worried?" There is humor in his voice, but there is also a little bit of accusation in his tone as well.

"Look, when you are a journalist, you have to be quick to think of scenarios and situations that will put you in the right place at the right time. It's not so much lying as it is strategic thinking, for the greater good of knowledge." His comment bothers her. Is it true? Does she compromise her ethics and her integrity to get stories? Is telling people she's getting community perspective a lie that she should feel remorse for, or is the fact that she is using the white lie as a means to finding the truth outweigh the immorality of the lie? She pushes her doubt to the back of her mind. Her drive to find what really happened is more important to her now. Hopefully no one will find them, and she won't have to tell a lie, or make an excuse.

They pull back into the circular drive and stop in front of the garage. Mason jumps out, leaving the truck running and jogs to the garage. His height makes it easy to look into the little windows along the top of the garage door. Addison, even with her height, would have needed a boost to see into the windows. Mason peers into a window, with his hands cupped to block the dwindling light. He moves along the length of the garage, which has four individual doors. Finally, at the furthest end, he stops and stands, peering for a few moments before turning around and returning to the car. His face is even more handsome with the serious look he wears. He hops back into the truck, "I think I found it. But it is all the way in the back of the garage, and there is a cover on it. I can't see if there's damage. Do you think I should see if one of the doors is open? That would definitely be crossing the line of what's right and wrong, I would be actively breaking and entering."

"No, I don't want you to break the law. I'm tempted, and I want to know too, but if we get caught, and we don't have any real evidence, we will both be in trouble. We'll lose our credibility. Then our hope of finding the person who hit Jamison will be lost, because no one will let us near them even if the police don't keep us in jail. I would say the fact that her beloved Jaguar is tucked into the back of her garage and covered is pretty good evidence that she is hiding something, especially in combination with the way she screeched out of the neighborhood when she saw us."

"Addison, before I pull out onto Georgetown Pike, are you sure we can leave and move on to the next stop?" He is teasing her, and she knows it.

"Yes, I think we've exhausted everything with Mrs. Anderson for now. Off to see Mr. Sayed." Mr. Sayed's neighbor had also supplied the name and address via Twittter. They head west down Georgetown Pike away from McLean for about three miles, and turn left onto Kimberwick Road. They pull into a more modest neighborhood, where the homes are traditional brick colonials or split levels, typical fifties development homes. Despite its much less grandiose feeling, the neighborhood is cozy, and kids are playing football outside in the front yard of one of the houses. The home they pull up to is a brick and white trimmed Cape Cod. It's neat and clean; there is a BMW in the driveway, as well as a Toyota minivan.

Mason helps Addison to the door and she rings the bell. Standing on the front stoop. They can smell the tangy spicy aroma of the meal being prepared in the home. A demure woman with graying hair opens the door; she is wearing an apron and wiping her hands on the front of it. "May I help you?" Despite her thick Indian accent, she is easy to understand.

"We are looking for Mr. Sayed. Is he here?"

"I'm afraid he is not home yet. May I ask what this is in regards to?"

"We are from the Chain Bridge High School News Magazine and we were hoping to speak to him about a story we are writing.

When would be a good time to return?"

"He should be home around seven. I'm not sure he will want to be disturbed."

"Could we leave our phone number with you? He could call us to plan a time when he would be available to meet. Would that be okay?"

"I suppose so, but I can't promise he will want to speak with you."

On the drive home, they call Campbell to see if there is any change with Jamison. Jamison is still in a coma, but his eyes are fluttering and his fingers have been twitching. The doctors have said that these could be signs of his brain slowly becoming more active, or they could be instinctual movements. Only time will tell if it is progress or natural movements. They promise Campbell that they will come see him on Thursday.

They head back to Addison's house to get their homework done. They are distracted from their work, thinking about Mrs. Anderson's strange behavior and the hidden car in her garage. Around eight that evening Addison's phone rings.

"Hello?" Addison answers, with a hopeful tone, wishing that it is Mr. Sayed.

"This is Mr. Sayed. I understand that you came by this afternoon looking for me."

"Yes, I'm Addison Erhard. My friend, Mason Gentry and I are writing a story for the school news magazine on the hit-and-run near your house. We were wondering if we could meet with you to ask some questions."

"May I ask why you would seek me out specifically?"

"We got a lead from a neighbor that you drive by the spot where the accident occurred every morning and we wanted to get your perspective of the road, its safety and how you think the accident could have been avoided."

"That is true, I do drive by there every morning on my way to McLean Racquet."

"Would you be able to meet in person?"

"I'm afraid not. I have a busy schedule. Can we do it now on the phone?"

"Sure, we have a few questions. I'm going to put the call on speaker, so that Mason can hear as well." She looks at Mason, who is intently trying to listen to Mr. Sayed through the phone. He nods his head as she places the phone on speaker. "What time do you normally drive down Georgetown Pike on Saturday mornings?" As Addison talks, Mason pulls out his own phone and sets it to record so that they will have a record of the call to go back to.

"I try to be at the gym in time for the 5:30 class, so usually I leave my house at 4:45."

"So, around five in the morning you are passing the area where Jamison was running?"

"Yes, ma'am."

"What's that part of the road like?"

"It is a difficult section, because there is a bend and it makes it difficult to see what's right beyond, especially because the trees grow right up to the side of the road."

"Do you come across runners on that portion of the road often?"

"Actually not often, especially because I'm out so early. Usually runners stay on the path, which is much safer."

"When you drove to the gym last Saturday, did you notice anything unusual? Based on the timing, you would have passed the area either shortly before or shortly after Jamison was hit."

"The only thing I remember was that there was still icy snow on the sidewalks, and that it was a foggy morning. A lot of the snow had melted the day before, and with the cooler evening temperatures, there was a heavy fog on the road. I never saw the runner, but that doesn't mean he wasn't out there."

"Do you believe that the city was responsible for the accident by not keeping the sidewalks clear?"

"To be perfectly honest, I do not believe that the young man should have been out running at that time of day, especially if the trails were not safe."

"In Jamison's defense, it is possible that the path was clear closer to his house, and that he didn't know that the trail was not going to be clear."

"That is possible. I have a hard time thinking it was the driver's fault. It could have easily have been me if my timing was off by a few moments." At this Mason and Addison look each other in the eye...would a guilty man make such a suggestion?"

"So you do not believe it was the driver's fault that Jamison was hit?"

"No, not that he was hit. However, the fact that the driver left the scene without making sure the runner was safe is unimaginable, especially because it wasn't the driver's fault. You can't expect a runner to appear out of nowhere on a cold March morning, running on the road when there is a path right there. But he or she should have stayed to make sure the runner was okay, and called 911 when it was apparent that he was not."

"Just to be clear, you didn't see anything on that road that morning?"

"No, ma'am. Is that all? I really have a lot to accomplish this evening."

"One last question. Do you know of anyone else who may have been driving along the road at the same time?"

"I suppose there are some more people who head down there towards the gym, but I wouldn't know specific names. I really need to go."

"Yes, sir, thank you so much for letting us interview you. We will send you a copy of the magazine when it is done."

"Good evening," Mr. Sayed hangs up the phone.

"I need some air. Do you want to go walk in the garden and we can talk about the interview with Mr. Sayed?"

"Sure. Are you going to be okay on the crutches?"

"Yeah, we can stay on the path. Chandler, wanna come?" Chandler behaves as if he has never heard anything better. He jumps and leaps as they grab light coats and head out through the sunroom to the garden. He races off in front of them, chasing some unseen prey. Addison realizes that he will probably be muddy and messy when he comes back. Her mother is not going to be happy with her.

Despite the fact that it is dark out, the path is lined with tiny lanterns that lead from the fence to her mom's studio, and along a smaller trail from the sunroom that joins the main path. There are additional smaller routes that meander from the main path to further and more secluded parts of the garden. Already ferns have started to break through the soil, and crocuses are bright along the mulch, with their white and purple blossoms peeking over grass-like leaves. Her mother has planted crocuses everywhere in the garden, so as soon as the weather starts to warm, they are the first to arrive, blanketing the garden with purple, yellow and white. They only last a few weeks, but it means that spring is finally here and that the winter is gone.

They walk along slowly, down the main path, their shoes and Addison's crutches crunch as they make their way. "So, what do you think?" Addison asks, looking up at Mason.

"I don't think he hit Jamison. He didn't have any nervousness to his voice. He was patient with our questioning."

"Yes, I sensed that too. Especially when he said that it could have been him just as easily. I don't think that someone who is guilty and trying to hide would bring that up."

"I agree, and unlike Mrs. Anderson, he didn't get angry with us when we dug a little deeper. He seems to believe that it was circumstances, that it could have happened to anyone."

"Except the 'run' part...he didn't seem to have much patience for the idea of leaving Jamison laying on the road, even if it wasn't the driver's fault."

"I would expect not too many people would condone leaving an injured person on the road."

"Yeah, you're right, that is normal human decency. I feel in my gut that it was Mrs. Anderson. She acted guiltily, she has a car she's hiding. How will we find enough proof to prove it?" She turns to Mason, looking up into his eyes. His short hair flutters in the breeze. He emanates kindness, understanding and security. He wraps his arms around her, and rests his head on the top of her head.

"We have to have faith that the truth will come out. I say we follow our instinct, that we keep an eye on Mrs. Anderson. If we don't see her Jaguar again, we alert Rodriguez. In the meantime, if we find any other leads, we follow them in the same way we did today." They stand in the garden together for a long time, letting the peaceful feeling of their private little corner, away from the chaos, stress and madness of Jamison's injury, protect them.

15
Heartbreak and Broken Dreams
Thursday, March 17

Late Thursday evening, after Mason has left to go back to his house, Addison lays in her bed with Chandler, reading a chapter for English. She suddenly has a powerful desire to talk to Campbell. In all her worry about finding out who hit Jamison, she has neglected Campbell, who has nearly lost one of her best friends. She texts her: *are you awake?*

Within a moment she sees the little floating dots showing that Campbell is writing her back. *Yep, can't sleep.*

Want to come sleep over here? I miss you.

Moments later: *on my way. Is it ok with your mom on a school night?* Addison quickly types back. *It's fine. she knows we need each other now.*

Addison clambers out of her bed and slips on her slippers and grabs her crutches. She hobbles down the hall to her parent's wing, and gently knocks on their suite door.

"Yes?"

"Can I come in?"

"Of course.'" Her mother's gentle voice already makes Addison feel better. It is amazing, that no matter how old she is, she still is calmed by her mother's voice. She opens the door and walks across the enormous bedroom to her parents' equally enormous bed. Her mother looks tiny, propped up against all her pillows. She's reading a well-worn, and obviously loved copy of *100 Years of Solitude*, by José Arcadio Buendía, Addison realizes how ironic that title is, as her mother is in bed alone, yet again, as her father works late into the night.

"Mom, Campbell and I are both really having a hard time with Jamison's accident. I know it is a school night, but I told Campbell she could come over and sleep here. I think we need each other's company. I'm sorry I didn't ask first, it felt like the right thing."

"Of course, Addie. How are you doing? I feel like with Mason around so much, I don't have a real opportunity to see how you are holding up." Her mom reaches out to smooth her hair, her eyes look deeply into Addison's. Addison feels like her mom is seeking the truth of her daughter's heart. Addison isn't completely sure herself what she thinks or how she is feeling.

"I'm stressed out. I've been so pre-occupied with Jamison and our investigation, I haven't had enough time or attention for school. It seems a bit meaningless to focus on studying equations when Jamison is in the hospital fighting to stay alive, and somewhere out here a person hit him, and got away with it."

"I know that it's true, and nothing is as important as your friend's life, but at the same time, Jamison wouldn't want you to sacrifice your future either. So take a break, but don't completely check out."

"I know, Mom. I'm not completely irresponsible. It's hard, that's all." She wishes she wouldn't snap like that; she knows she's lucky her mom supports her so much...but her mom gets under her skin so quickly. "I'm going downstairs to wait for Cams. Thanks for letting her stay, it means a lot to both of us."

"I know honey. Let me know if you need anything from me."

"Okay. Love you." She turns awkwardly with her crutches and makes her way along the hall and down the stairs. She curls up in the window seat overlooking the front drive. After a few minutes, she sees Campbell's old Ford Taurus pull into the driveway and park in front of the house. While she is thinking of it, she texts Mason to let him know that she won't need to be picked up in the morning. She's looking forward to being with Campbell for a few hours, just the two of them, like it always used to be. She misses her buddy. She can't believe how having a boyfriend has changed her priorities. She wonders if Campbell has resented Mason at all, or if Jamison took over her place completely. She imagines how hard it must be for her, with Jamison hurt and possibly dying, and Addison physically and emotionally absent with Mason. She promises herself that she will be a better friend to Campbell.

Campbell struggles up the front steps with her overnight bag, her book bag and her lunch box. She comes crashing through the doorway, and Chandler nearly loses his mind in excitement, completely convinced that Campbell is there exclusively for him.

"Hey, Cams. I wish I could help you, but with these crutches I'm pretty much worthless...Is it okay that I called off Mason for my morning ride? You'll be stuck with my stuff too." She looks at Campbell with sheepish eyes. She hates how her injury is causing everyone around her more work.

"Ummm...can't Mason pick us both up and carry all our stuff? I'm going to herniate a disk." Campbell squints her eyes and grabs for her lower back in mock pain.

"Do you want me to ask him? You know he would."

"Nah. I don't want to share you tomorrow. I want to go together, run by Starbucks before school — like the good ole days. We might have to build in an extra few minutes for me to ferry in all our crap."

"How about I ask him to meet up in the parking lot. He can be our pack mule."

"Great thinking."

It feels good to be silly and light-hearted again. Even though it has not even been a week, the last few days have been so stressful, and so life changing, it feels like a lifetime ago that her biggest concern was her performance at regionals. Now she wishes she could go back to her innocent one-week-younger self. It's stunning how fast a person's life can change.

"Let's go settle in upstairs. I still have a little reading to do, you?"

"Yes. Stupid English reading. Seriously, I can't imagine how people can enjoy *Beowulf*."

"Oh, I'm such an English nerd. I love mythology, and especially Norse."

"Well, maybe you can read it to me and help me understand what the heck is going on."

They make their way into Addison's bedroom. She is already in her pajamas, and settles right in. As she always does, Campbell takes the right side of the bed, and makes herself comfortable. "Did you see Jamison today?"

"I did. It is so sad Addie. He's wearing that horrendous mask, and his eyes are closed. He looks so fragile, nothing like the vibrant and outgoing Jamison I know and love."

"I know. It's heartbreaking. I'll go with you tomorrow if you want me to. I know it must be hard to sit there day after day, waiting and alone."

"That would be really nice. He actually was moving his fingers today, and he seemed to be responding to loud sounds, and when they tapped him on his feet. I feel him coming back to me. I keep saying 'Come back to me Jamison.' I swear, if he wasn't gay I would offer to marry him if he would wake up for me." Campbell smiles through tears that are brimming in her eyes.

"How have his parents been?" Addison knows that his parents weren't fully supportive or acceptant of his being gay. She wonders if this will help them see past that, accept him just as he is, as long as he lives.

"You know, the silver lining in all this is that I think they could care less if he's gay, if he goes into the Peace Corps, or if he becomes a gypsy. They love him and they want him back, at any cost and any price. My biggest fear is that he will come back, but he won't be Jamison; he will be some sort of shadow of himself."

"I've actually done a bit of research. Studies say that some head injury patients may recover slowly, but it means that their brains are so busy rebuilding. I imagine him with his eyes closed and serene; meanwhile inside his head, all these little neurons and electrodes are rebuilding, and that he will wake up in a few weeks and be even better than he was before the accident."

"I hope you're right, Addie. I can't imagine a life without Jamison in it."

"Want me to read *Beowulf* to you? It's about how a man overcomes a huge creature, against all the odds. That's our Jamison. Against all odds."

The next morning Campbell wakes Addison up at the unimaginable time of 4:30 so that they can get dressed, pack up the car and make it to Starbucks and school in time to meet Mason in the parking lot at seven o'clock. As Mason loads up Addison's bags, they make plans for the weekend.

"What are you planning on doing this weekend, Campbell?" Mason asks, pulling Addison's backpack over his right shoulder, balancing his own bag on his left. Against Mason's enormous back, her bag looks small and light. Despite her pleasure in having an excuse to see Mason between each class and every morning, she can't wait to be independent enough to carry her own bags again. It's crazy how being injured makes small little habits, like carrying your stuff, become treasured symbols of independence and strength. She wonders how long it will be for Jamison to become self-sufficient again, if he ever does.

"I have an indoor soccer tournament, and I suppose I'll spend time at the hospital with Jamison. It's been really hard on his parents, watching over him; I've been trying to spend a lot of time with him on the weekends so that they can go home and rest." As Campbell says this, Addison wonders if she will ever take the time to take care of herself. She looks tired and has big bags under her eyes; her clothes look like they came out of a bag, which they did, and her hair is in a messy pony tail.

"Campbell, have you thought about taking some rest time off for yourself? A little time away from school and the hospital to relax?"

"It doesn't seem fair to think about myself when Jamison is laying in the hospital."

"Well, it won't make him happy to know you've worked yourself to death worrying and caring for him either, Cams." Addison looks at her with concern in her eyes." He needs you to be rested when he wakes up, not a sleepwalking zombie."

"I have an idea," says Mason from behind. "What if we all spend the day at the farm on Sunday? We could ride horses and work around the farm a bit. I know it sounds like it wouldn't be fun, but honestly working on the farm and the animals is the best for a person's soul. It's peaceful, you can think; it helps me each time I'm overwhelmed. I bet we can think through the accident and what we know, maybe even figure it out."

"That sounds perfect to me…. Cams? What do you think?"

"I think it sounds good. I have to check with my parents first, and I have to see how much homework I have. I can't go if it will put me behind in my work."

"Check with your mom and let us know, okay?" Campbell walks off to class and Mason and Addison head towards her math class.

"I hope that you come to the farm either way. It would be nice to have you stay there and spend time with my mom and dad, and work on the farm for a day or two.

"I need to see how my hamstring is. I've an appointment today after school. I can't imagine that my mom will let me go out to the farm if I'm still on crutches. I can't ride horses or make my way around the farm like an invalid."

That afternoon Addison's mom picks her up from school and they head to the doctor's office. She is tired of being an invalid on crutches; she hopes that the doctor will let her walk. She has worked so hard at being a good patient; she prays that she will receive good news.

The doctor's office is drab and depressing. The walls are painted a muted pea green, which was probably a vibrant pea green in the seventies when it was last painted. The scuffed linoleum floors are gray, dull and smell of Pinesol cleaner. In order to compensate for the chilly spring weather outside, the air is hot and dry in the office, making Addison even more miserable sitting in the cheap pleather chairs. Her mother looks equally wretched, fanning herself with an old copy of *People* magazine, which has long since lost its appeal, with its cover of Angelina Jolie and her brood and its claim that her life is falling apart, yet again.

After forty-five minutes of waiting, Addison and her mother are finally ushered into the office. After a brief visit with the doctor, x-rays and an ultrasound are ordered. The x-ray to see if any chips of bone have detached with the muscle, and the ultrasound to see the extent of the tear and swelling. Another forty-five minutes go by before the doctor comes in again to tell her that she needs to stay off her leg for another few days to make sure that the hamstring properly heals, icing and elevating as much as possible, especially if she wants to continue in her running career. She also needs to continue her therapy with some stretching with a band under the guidance of her physical therapist.

Dejected, Addison and her mother return to the car. "Mom, I don't know how much longer I can bear being on my crutches. I feel so helpless. I want to be able to carry my own things, I want to be able to investigate Jamison's accident, and I want to help Mason on his farm. It isn't fair!" All the pressure, fear and disappointment that Addison has been feeling the last months well up in her heart. She feels them bubble from deep in her gut, through her chest and finally escape in hot, frustrated tears. Her mom places her arms around her daughter, soothing her, patting her back and stroking her hair.

"I know, sweet girl. This is so frustrating and difficult for you. I'm so sorry. I wish I could make it go away, but all I can do is support you and love you, baby girl. Shhhhh, Shhhhhh."

Slowly her sobs slow down and stop choking her. She takes several deep breaths and leans heavily into her mother's embrace. "Thank you, Mom. I love you. Thanks for standing by me and being here for me."

"Do you want to stop at Greenberry's and pick up a coffee and a treat?" She and her mom have a tradition of stopping in at the local coffee shop whenever they have been to the doctor or the dentist. It was a tradition started when Addison was a little girl. They would come in and Addison would order a small hot chocolate, especially prepared for a child, lukewarm, with a gigantic oatmeal raisin cookie, and her mother would have her Americano, an espresso drink mixed with hot water. They would nibble the cookie together. During the summer months they would sit outside on the patio and watch McLean residents, including senators and diplomats come and go, ordering their fine coffee drinks. As she grew up, Addison developed a taste for coffee, preferring a cappuccino, with the frothy milk floating over the top.

"Yeah, a coffee sounds perfect."

They drive the few blocks to Greenberry's and park the car in between the Audis and Mercedes typical to the suburb. They walk through the afternoon sun and into the coffee shop. Despite the lateness of the day, the sun is still warm. Addison's dark mood starts to lift as she realizes that the end of the winter is really here, and that the days will continue to grow warmer and longer. She looks along the sidewalks and sees the tiny little leaves of the crocus and tulips poking through mulch. Maybe things will get better soon.

That evening, Mason comes over again. They sit together in the basement to watch a movie and munch on popcorn. Addison's basement is enormous. Her parents have the "adult" area, where there is a full kitchen, stocked with food and drinks. Her parents often entertain there, watching sporting events on the big-screen television mounted along the seating area. On the other side of the basement is a home gym and a guest room, with a full bath. She and Mason are in the movie viewing room, which is dark, and has a projection TV, an enormous chocolate brown sectional where she and Mason sit. She nestles cozily in the crook of his arm, leaning into his chest as they watch *Hunger Games*. Addison loves Katniss; she feels that they have a similar rebellious and fighting attitude. Gale reminds her of her own Mason. She doesn't understand why Katniss doesn't run off with Gale right at the start of the movie...she would.

As they sit together, Mason gently strokes Addison's shoulder and her arms are wrapped around his broad chest. With her ear against his chest, she can hear him breathing, in and out, his heart beating strong and rhythmically, consistent and resilient, just as he has been through all of this. "Mason, do you think this is all going to work itself out?" she whispers as the movie comes to an end.

His deep voice vibrates through his body, "Yep, I do. I think Jamison is gonna pull through. I think he's gonna wake up and it may take a while. But he's coming back. I feel it in my bones."

"I hope you're right, Mason," she breathes. Deep down she does feel like he will come back, but she also has a pit in her stomach about something else. "Do you think that we will find the driver of the car? Maybe Jamison will wake up and remember."

"I doubt it, honestly. It's so hard to track down the driver if there is no witness. And with Jamison's coma, the likelihood that he will remember the accident at all is so small. Then he would need to have seen and be able to recall the car and driver — remember, it was dark, it's unlikely. I think we need to admit that he or she got away with it. The only way they will be charged is if they come forward, and why haven't they already?

"Maybe our approach to Mrs. Anderson should be to threaten to expose and pressure her to admit that she was the one driving the car." Addison's brow is furrowed. She is feeling hopeless and frustrated. Part of her is angry with Mason for even suggesting that they should give up so early in the game.

"But we don't know she did it, babe. We don't have any evidence. Is it right to pressure someone in the hopes that we're right? Won't that be wrong, to harass her if she's innocent? I think the best we can do is let Rodriquez know what we learned and let the police take it from here. If they think there is enough suspicion to talk to her, or to ask to see her jaguar, they will."

"I'm frustrated. How can there be nothing we can do?!" Addison is sitting up now, moving away from Mason. She can't give in. She can't give up. She's like Katniss, isn't she? "I won't give up, there has to be something we're missing. I will continue to look for an answer until we find something. If Jamison does wake up, I pray he knows exactly who did this. I hope he has a crystal clear memory."

"Okay, okay babe, don't get angry with me...I'm not the one who hit Jamison! Let's go visit him tomorrow, and then let's take a small break and go to the farm on Sunday. We'll stay in the main area of the farm, like the barn, so that you don't have to worry about the crutches. Maybe we can take the dune buggy out to get some fresh air. Then Monday, we start doing more investigating and research. Maybe what we need is a little break from the stress and the area, get out, come back with a fresh mind and fresh eyes."

"Okay, but if you break me on the dune buggy and keep me on these stupid crutches, I'll kill you!" She hits him with a pillow, and then leans back into his embrace. "You always know what to say to make me see straight. I love you, Mason." It is the first time she has said this. She has felt it, she has meant it, but she has not said it before. She holds her breath, worried that Mason doesn't feel the same about her. He takes her face in his hands; he looks into her emerald eyes, dark with emotion, and leans his face close to hers. He gently kisses her lips and electricity runs through her from her head to her toes. Every part of her responds to Mason. She is amazed how his presence and his touch set her on fire. She wraps her arms around him tighter and disappears into his kiss.

16

Field of Dreams

Saturday, March 18

The next morning Addison wakes up; there is a text waiting for her from Campbell. She wants to go and see Jamison. He was more responsive yesterday and Campbell is excited and hopeful that this is a sign that he is coming back soon. She calls Mason to see if he wants to come have breakfast and then drive her to see Jamison. She hates that she always needs a ride; she misses her independence. However, she reminds herself that these are probably the last few days on her crutches, if she can be good, ice it, stretch it, and rest it.

After a quick breakfast of bagels and coffee with Addison's mom, Addison and Mason take their coffees to go and head to the hospital to meet Campbell. The drive to Georgetown Hospital is about eight miles from Addison's house; about a twenty-minute drive. The hospital sits at the top of a cliff along the Potomac River, on the outskirts of Washington, D.C., and is part of Georgetown University. As she and Mason drive along Chain Bridge Road and then Canal Road, Addison is struck by the beauty of her city. Perhaps it's because she knows that Jamison may never see this again, or the fact that her injury has caused her to re-evaluate what really matters to her; either way, she is enjoying seeing her surroundings through a new filter.

The river runs rapid under Chain Bridge as they cross from

Virginia into Washington D.C. Along the Virginian side the cliffs stand tall, with the most expensive and elaborate McLean houses over-looking the river. In the water, gray boulders stick out, causing the water to rush around them, creating wild white water. On this March morning a few adventurous souls are out in their white water kayaks braving not only the water, but the cold. Addison glances over at Mason's console to see that this morning the temperature is fifty-eight, which is relatively warm for a March morning. She guesses that today's high will be in the 60s, which brings her a new surge of joy, the feeling that things are getting better, that the world is renewing, and perhaps so are things in her life. Her leg is healing, Jamison is waking up, and she and Mason are closer than ever, relying on one another for strength, a partnership in this crazy life.

As they cross the river, they enter D.C., Along Canal Road runs the C&O Canal and its trail, which extends 185 miles from Georgetown all the way to Cumberland, Maryland. Addison doesn't know anyone who has biked the entire trail, but she knows people do. Today, taking advantage of the beautiful spring morning, runners and cyclists are crowding the gravel trail. She watches them with envy, and can't wait to run again, the urge is almost painful, as she looks down at her leg, knowing that the hamstring is torn and slowly healing. "Mason, when my leg is better, can we come down here and go for a run together? Looking at these runners makes me physically pained. I can't wait to get out there again."

"Sure, Angel, we can make it your first run back. It's perfect, flat, gravel, no cars to worry about. It would be perfect." He looks over at her as they drive, and his brown eyes are warm and caring, "I would love nothing more than to go out on your first run with you."

When they arrive at the hospital, they find that Campbell is already in the room with Jamison. It feels differently here than the last time they visited Jamison; it is no longer cold, terrifying and imposing. The atmosphere has changed to something less horrific and dark; there is an air of hope in the room today. She notices immediately that Jamison's skin looks more vibrant, his dark skin having lost its gray pallor. As Addison and Mason find chairs to sit in, Jamison stirs.

"That is exactly what I was talking about," says Campbell excitedly. "I think he sensed you coming in. Didn't you see him react?" Her excitement is palpable.

"It's a good sign, right?" Addison asks, "I read that as coma patient starts to heal and come out of it, they stir slightly, react to sounds and touch. Do you know if they have poked his feet to see if he responded?

"They did and he did move, a little, but they said it was a definite reaction to the pain. They can't tell yet if it's voluntary or just subconscious."

"Have the doctors given any prognosis, or what we can expect next? Will he wake up?" Mason asks, with trepidation in his voice. Addison assumes that Mason is afraid to have too much hope, to believe in Jamison's recovery, when really there is no way to predict if a coma patient will fully come out of it, and if they do wake up, how much of the original person, their memories and their personality, will remain.

"They don't know. It's so frustrating. I feel like we know as much as they do. How can they have attended eight years of medical school, practiced medicine for years have all their fancy machines and still not know what will happen to our Jamison, and if he's coming back or not!?" The frustration in Campbell's voice is evident. She looks tired, with dark bags under her eyes, and her hair is in its normal pony tail, only it is messier and greasier than usual. Her face looks drawn and tired.

"Campbell, can you get away with us for a little while tomorrow? We're going to Mason's place to ride the dune buggy, see the horses, you know, hang out and relax. I bet you don't even know what that is anymore."

"Okay, I'll do it, even if I should be home doing homework. I need to get away…. wait. What if Jamison wakes up? Shouldn't we be here?"

"If he wakes up, his parents are going to want to be here with him. Alone. If he doesn't wake up, you don't miss anything. Just come already."

"Okay. I will. What time do I need to be ready?"

The early morning drive to Marshall is a beautiful one. Once they leave the urban ring, the rolling hills are covered with bright green grasses as they wake up from the cold winter months. The trees are still bare, but the pine trees scattered throughout the forests give the hills the green they need to indicate spring is near. Along 66, the median grasses and those along the road are speckled with daffodils and crocuses. The sun is bright and warm, giving Addison hope and a feeling of contentment for the first time in what seems like months. She is sitting in the truck next to Mason, whom she has now said she loves, and in the back seat is her best friend. The empty seat next to Campbell makes her miss Jamison, but seeing his movement yesterday makes her have more faith in his recovery than she's had since his accident.

Mason guides the truck off the freeway and along the exit to seventeen. They head down 17 and through the tiny town of Marshall and onto 55, leaving the town behind, passing old homes that line the road. After another fifteen minutes of turning onto increasingly smaller roads, they pull up to Aberdale Farm, Mason's home. They turn onto the long gravel drive and pass through the stone gates, entering the property. The drive is lined with tall trees, and at the far end stands the imposing farmhouse. Mason slows the truck down and drives carefully up to the house.

"You never know which insane or stupid dog might run up to the truck. Unfortunately, it's survival of the fittest out here, and not all the dogs are smart enough to see that the truck is bigger than they are," laughs Mason. As if on cue, three large lab mix dogs come running out from the trees and shrubs excitedly greeting them.

"Do you think they know your truck?" asks Campbell.

"Yeah, they're wagging their tails, theirs are barks of excitement. They are much fiercer when they don't know the truck. A friend of my dad's sat in his car a good ten minutes before he called us from the car to remove the dogs"

Although Addison has seen the farm before, that was in the

dark and from afar. She did not fully understand the beauty of it and its surrounding areas. The big yellow farmhouse looks bright, yet retains the quaintness in its age. By no means does it appear old in terms of run-down, but old in the way that there is history in its walls, in the shutters that frame the windows and the beautifully manicured garden. Just as they had seen on the ride in, the farm is surrounded by an ancient fence made of the rocks its original owners had pulled from the earth as they farmed the land for the first time. It amazes Addison as she looks at the immense length of the fence that so many rocks could have been lodged in the earth, which now looks soft with a fresh new grass growing in clumps, some thicker patches where the sun and earth are richest.

Mason easily parks his huge truck in front of the barn, next to a much older Chevy pick-up, covered in rust. It is obviously old, its frame is white, yet there are two mismatched doors, one blue and one red. The bed is loaded with bales of hay. "Mason, what's up with the truck? How come you don't drive that one to McLean?" Campbell asks with humor in her voice.

"That's my grandpa's old truck. My dad can't get himself to get rid of it. He keeps replacing parts; as you can see he couldn't find two white doors at the junkyard. As long as he can keep it running and find more parts in the junkyard, that truck will be here. Whether it could make the drive to McLean is another matter. Not to mention that the truck's ugliness wouldn't survive next to the Audis and Beemers at Chain Bridge! It would wither in shame."

As he places his truck in park and gets out, Mason comes around to help Addison swing her long and encumbered legs from the truck and hands her the crutches. Mrs. Gentry opens the kitchen door, drying her hands in her apron. She is a handsome woman, both strong and beautiful at once. Her graying black hair is swept back into a simple bun, her face has classic beauty, with strong cheekbones and a long straight nose; however, there is no delicacy to her features. Addison can see the same features in his mother that makes Mason's features so strong and masculine. It is almost unnerving to see the same features in his mother's face.

"Welcome to the farm, girls! I'm so happy that Mason was able to convince you to make the trek out to Aberdale. Addison, I'm so please to finally meet you. Hope y'all are hungry! I finished making you kids some brunch. Eggs, bacon and sausage, grits and biscuits. Come on in!" Mason's mom has an even stronger Southern accent than her son, making Addison think of *Gone with the Wind*, she can imagine a younger version of his mother standing on their front porch drinking sweet tea and entertaining suitors.

As they walk towards the house, Mason whispers, "You don't have to eat it all. My mom will try to feed you until you burst. We don't allow her near the animals for fear they will eat until they literally die. But, what you do eat will make her day!"

"Okay! Luckily I'm starving, I may eat her out of house and home!" Addison is hungry, she was too late getting ready this morning to grab anything to eat other than the coffees she made them for the drive. She has heard her stomach growling for the last thirty minutes of the drive.

As they walk into the kitchen, Addison sees that the old age of the house is on the limited primarily to the outside. The kitchen has been completely renovated, although it maintains the charm of the age of the house. The floor is made of thick and wide dark wooden planks. The kitchen is enormous, as if the Gentrys feed a family of ten on a daily basis. In the center is a large island with a butcher top, where Mason's mom can roll out dough for pies and cookies. It smells as if she has been doing both. Along the four walls are off-white distressed cabinets, which look like they may have originally belonged to the house. The sink is a classic apron sink, with a porcelain front that dips low, ending above the doors to the cabinet beneath it. The faucets are made of copper and shine as if they are new, or recently polished. The stove gives away that this is a newer remodeled kitchen, as it is an "antique" Bertazzoni range, burgundy with chrome. It's shiny and expensive looking, indicating that despite wanting the kitchen to look original to the home, Mason's mom and dad don't want to cook like old fashioned farmers.

Along the island are five bar stools. "Come, have a seat, kids. I will put the breakfast out. Your dad ate early this morning before heading out, Mason." Addison pulls her long caramel hair back behind her shoulders as she pulls a stool out. She leaves a seat on either side of her, one for Mason and one Campbell. So far the day has been wonderful, and she has enjoyed Campbell coming along, but she feels jealously creeping up inside her, and she feels a desire to keep Mason to herself. Putting Campbell to the left, and Mason to her right will allow her a little bit of a monopoly on Mason's time, at minimum of his body. She pats the chair to her right, "Mason, have a seat, babe." He sits down next to her, his broad shoulders and thick thighs pushing against her, as they sit at the end, with tiny little Campbell perched on the stool to the left of them both.

"So, what are you three kids going to do today? Riding the horses?"

"Well, Addie can't ride yet, so I thought we'd take out the dune buggy and give the girls a tour of the land, or at least the parts we can easily reach on the buggy. I've promised Addison that I won't risk injuring her leg. I think she would literally kill me if I did that." Mason's mom looks at Addison with the same dark brown eyes as her son, both sets of eyes shining with humor.

"You know I would too, not to mention what my dad would do to you if you broke me!" Addison playfully hits Mason on the shoulder and turns to Campbell. "Cams, if you really want to ride the horses you can. I don't want my injury to hold you both back."

"Ummm, no. Not getting on a horse. Horses and I don't get along well. I love the *idea* of riding a horse, but the one time I got on one at my friend's birthday party, mind you it was a pony, not even a real horse, I slid right off it. Like, I mean the guy put me up on the horse from the right and I literally slid right off the other side. I sat on that pony for a split second. It was a mutual decision between me and the pony that we should end the relationship then and there. So, a dune buggy sounds great."

As they chat, Mason's mom heaps plates full of the breakfast she has promised. They eat heartily, joking and teasing, and simply relaxing. Addison can feel the tension of the last few weeks melting away, out here in the country, in a kitchen that feels like part of the past, being spoiled by Mason's mom. After none of them can eat another bite, they get up, sloth-like, from the island and head outside. By now it is almost noon, and the sun is high up in the sky. It is a beautiful day, the sky is a crisp clear blue, with no wind to be felt. The air feels fresh and warm, and they shed their outer layers and throw them in the truck.

"Let's head into the barn and have a peek at the horses. Campbell, I promise I won't make you touch them, but they will resent me if I come this close and don't pay them a visit."

"They would know you were here?" Addison asks with doubt in her voice.

"Absolutely, you think the hounds know me? They are dumb as a box of rocks compared to the horses. You know how you can wrong a dog and he will forget two seconds later that you were mean and start wagging his tail again? The horses are the opposite. You slight a horse, and she will hold a grudge against you for years to come. I'm not kidding."

"Which horse is yours?" Campbell asked.

"This big chestnut mare, Acorn. My dad got her for me when I turned twelve — you can tell by the name I gave her, not so creative. He made me train her myself. Said it would teach me more about the importance of discipline than any punishment he could ever give me. He was right. She taught me how important it is to follow the rules and to be consistent. A horse appreciates a person who is predictable and reliable."

"So I have her to thank — thank you, Acorn." Addison gently strokes the mare; whose eyes are as dark brown as her master's. She is gentle and kind, and Addison can feel this from stroking her. Her muscles are relaxed as she nuzzles into Addison's hand. "I think that Acorn is the true love of your life." As soon as she says these words she regrets them. She has put Mason in a place where he has to respond. He either has to profess her as the love of his life, or he has to reject her as his true love, and choose his horse.

"There is only real girl for me. I find Acorn a little lacking in the conversation department. It always seems so one-sided, know what I mean?" Addison sighs with relief. Of course he made joke of it. Just as she feels this relief, Mason envelopes her in his arms. "I meant it, Angel," he whispers into her ear, quickly kissing her neck. She looks into his eyes, "I know."

"Awkward third wheel here...speaking of wheels...what are these messy tires doing here?" She is tugging at a tarp over a stack of tires, which are taller than she. Grimacing with disgust at the tires, muddy and perhaps with even a little manure on them, she looks at Mason with inquiring eyes.

"Oh those, they are my winter tires. I guess I never put them in the attic like I should have. Dad's going to whip me if he finds out. Hey, I'll move them up now. Do you guys want to go look at the other horses in the pasture outside? Luna is a sweet young one. She's the tan quarter horse with a brown face. She's gentle. Her dad, Stormy, is the gray one. Watch out for him, he'll nip at you. I won't be more than a minute."

The girls head out to the pasture. "It's so beautiful here. It feels like we are in a completely different world, a different time, a different dimension. His mom is ridiculously nice. She reminds me of Eric Foreman's mom from *That 70's show*. I bet when his dad comes home she has his slippers and drink ready," says Campbell partially impressed and partially horrified.

"It's crazy; I don't know how Mason goes from our McLean world to this one. They are so different. It would be confusing."

"Or maybe it would be a relief, a way to survive the pressure and the stress. You come out here on the weekends and forget that all the craziness, pressure and demands exist at all. You come back refreshed and ready for the week. Addie, I'm gonna be honest with you, where is this going? You seem smitten with him, but I don't see you living out in Marshall. This is as far from New York as Pluto is from Earth. You are no Mrs. Gentry. No offense to her, or you."

"I know. I know. I love him, Cams. I feel it so strongly. But I couldn't live here and he would die in New York. I feel like it won't work, but it's so much fun for now. I can't imagine my life without him. I mean, seriously, we have another eighteen months before we all leave for college. Anything could happen. I'm living in the moment."

"I'm your best friend Addie. I've known you since we were four. You don't live in the moment, you're a planner. I mean, you have planned to be a journalist and travel the world for, like, ever. You know what you're eating, who you will see, and which assignments you will finish, and when. You probably have your reading assignments broken down by pages per day, don't you?"

"Yes…"

"Then this will not work for you. If you stay with Mason, you will sell out. You love him and I know you, you will be invested in him."

"If it's meant to be..."

"That's not you, Addie. It just isn't."

"Maybe love changes you; maybe love is enough to make us both change." Addison thinks again about her mother and father, and the love her mother thought was enough to accept a secret that went against everything she believed in. Was it really enough?

"Hey girls." Addison and Campbell turn around, startled to see Mason standing there. Addison wonders if he heard their conversation. His eyes are shielded with concern. His voice is curt. She wishes Campbell had kept her concerns to herself. If Mason overheard them, will he doubt her love for him?

For the rest of the day, Mason seems withdrawn. If Addison could go back and erase the conversation from existence, she would. Only she can't. Mason heard it, but more concerning, Campbell brought up the doubts Addison has hidden further and further in the depths of her heart as she has fallen deeper into love with Mason. The conversation has brought it to the forefront. She has to face the fact that in the long run, she and Mason are not compatible; unless she is willing to give up her dream of becoming a traveling journalist, or Mason is willing to give up his dream of farming his families land.

17
Twists and Turns Along the Path
Monday, March 20

On Monday, Campbell gets a phone call from Jamison's mom. Jamison has woken up. He is not speaking, but his eyes are open and he is responsive to his environment. He seems confused and disoriented, which is to be expected. Jamison's mom has asked that they wait a few days to visit, to give him time to adjust, and to keep the new stimulation at a minimum. She promises Campbell that they will be the first non-family members to see Jamison. She will call when they are ready.

On Tuesday morning, before school, Jamison's mom calls Campbell and tells her that she can bring Addison and Mason to see Jamison after school. She asks them to be quiet, and to let Jamison adjust to them slowly. She says that he may not recognize them, and that may be frightening to them all. She suggests that they come in individually, giving Jamison time to adjust to each one.

After school, Campbell meets Addison and Mason in the parking lot of Georgetown Hospital. Today is warm again, but it is cloudy and has been raining off and on all day. Despite the warm weather, Addison feels a chill down her spine. She can't figure out if she is nervous for Jamison's reaction to them, to see if he remembers who they are and why they are there, or if the journalist in her wants to see if Jamison will have remembered what

177

happened to him — or has any information about the accident. Since the trail has run cold, Addison has had a restless feeling that there is more to the story. She's written her article about the accident and Jamison's recovery, without naming her suspect. She's explained how they did their research and what they found. It's frustrating to have the story end without an answer. She reminds herself that concussion and brain injury patients often lose their memory of the accident. The chances of Jamison being able to recall the information is minimal, and even then — if he was even aware of being hit, let alone by whom.

Addison's physical therapist and orthopedist have released Addison from her crutches, finally. She can walk on her own, and as she climbs out of the truck without Mason's help; she feels a pride in her independence. It makes her appreciate a body that works. She wonders how much help Jamison is going to need, and how long the physical recovery is going to be for him. His injuries are a hundred times worse than hers. She can't even begin to imagine what that would do to your sense of independence. Mason reaches for her hand as they walk towards Campbell. Campbell, who is waiting impatiently for them to arrive. Campbell who has been sitting vigilantly next to Jamison these long days. Campbell who has had faith in Jamison's recovery. She is bursting with excitement and joy.

"I can't believe it, guys! The day is finally here. I know he's going to be okay now. I mean, I know it's going to be a long road but with us he can do this! I can't wait to see him. Do you think he will recognize us? Remember that if he doesn't, it means he needs more time, it will be okay." All of this is said in a long stream and in one breath. Campbell is about to explode.

"Cams, calm down, girl. You can't go in there all hyped up. That is not going to help him keep calm. He'll have a stroke if you come in there bouncing around and babbling a mile a minute." Addison puts a soothing arm around Campbell. She is so tense her body is shaking like a leaf. "Maybe we should sit down for a minute and make a plan."

Mason takes her by arm and leads her away from the door. "Good idea, here, Campbell. Let's sit on this bench. So, I think you should go in first. But you gotta promise us that you won't say a word. Not one word. Just go in, sit next to him, and if you can, hold his hand. After three minutes of saying nothing, you can say, "Hey, Jamison, it's me, Campbell," and let him adjust to that news. Take the cues from him. After about ten minutes, Addison will come in, and she will sit next to you, same drill, quietly, let him adjust and then she'll remind him of who she is. Sound good so far?"

Campbell takes a deep, calming breath. Her small heart-shaped face works hard to relax and void itself of emotion. She looks into Mason's eyes, and then Addison's, "Yes, I can do that. When do you come in, Mason?"

"If all goes well, I will come in last. I don't want to freak him out. He knows me the least of us all. I'll wait for a cue from Addie. If he has reacted to you well, I'll come in after you; same drill, sit, wait and then I'll remind him that it's me."

"Okay, I can do this; we can do this. I don't know what I will do if he gives me a blank stare."

Addison faces Campbell and reaches over and draws a strand of her dark blonde hair away from her eyes; she takes Campbell's face in both her hands. "Then you will continue to sit by his side and be there for him. Jamison is going to come back to us. You may need to be patient a little longer."

"Okay, let's go, girls," says Mason, standing up tall, pulling each girl with one hand. Addison feels his strength flow from his arm into hers. His confidence and his plan have calmed them all.

When they get to Jamison's room, they see his mother's back facing them, blocking their view of Jamison. She turns when she hears them approach and quickly comes to the hall, closing the door behind her. Her face is tired; her graying hair seems to have gone grayer these last few weeks; but there is also relief written over her face. "Hey, kids," she says as she grasps each of their hands one by one. "Thank you so much for coming. You have been here for him in so many ways, and for us too. He is doing well; the doctors are pleased with his response to us. Even though he can't speak, he seems to recognize us. I've told him what happened, and he seems to understand. He has only seen his immediate family so far. You are the first non-family to see him. The doctors are actually interested to see how he reacts to you all, so they will be observing from the window."

"Okay, we thought it would be good for us to walk in one at a time. Give him some time to adjust before another comes in. What do you think?" Campbell looks into her eyes, with hope that this suggestion is a good one.

"That sounds ideal to me. Campbell, I hope you will go in first."

"Yes, me, then Addie and then Mason. Mason will only go in if Jamison responds to us well. He doesn't want to distress Jamison with too many new faces."

"Okay, sounds good. I'm going to sit in the corner. I hope you understand that I don't want to let him out of my sight for a little while."

"Of course!" Campbell gives Mrs. Randolph a quick hug and follows her into the room. Addison and Mason watch as she sits down next to Jamison and holds his hand. Her back blocks Jamison's face from their view, so they cannot see his reaction. They can see Campbell wipe tears away from her face, and they see her hold his hand. After a few minutes she leans in close and whispers her name in his ear. Again, she wipes tears from her face. She turns in her chair and beckons for Addison to come and sit with her.

Addison sits down next to Campbell. Jamison's face is full of expression. She can tell that he has recognized them. Relief floods through her body. His eyes are his. He is Jamison in those deep dark eyes. His twinkle is there; how can he possibly be back so soon? He shifts his hand towards her. She grabs it gently, trying not to touch the IV cable that is strapped to it. His hand is warm and she can feel a difference from the last time she held it. It was placid; now she can feel the muscles react to her touch. She gently strokes the palm of his hand and leans in closer to whisper, "Hey, Jamison, it's me, Addie. It's so good to see you awake." His hand squeezes hers, and it is with all the willpower she possesses that she doesn't jump up with joy and hug him. She stays her body and holds his hand as she looks at Campbell. It is then that she sees that Campbell has been watching her closely, to watch her reaction to Jamison.

"He knows us," she whispers in an almost inaudible voice. Tears streaming down her face.

They both turn to Mason and beckon him in. Mason comes in slowly and pulls a chair ever so quietly to sit next to Addison. His face is downturned. He looks at the ground, busies himself with the chair and looks around the room, at the window with the doctor's observing, at Jamison's mom, sitting quietly in the corner observing her son ever so carefully. Addison feels like he is afraid of seeing Jamison, is avoiding him. She can't blame him; she was terrified that he wouldn't recognize her.

Finally, Mason looks at Jamison. Campbell and Addison both look to Jamison's face to see if he also recognizes Mason. The look on Jamison's face is recognition, but it is more than that. They see shock; they see terror. They look back at Mason, and he reflects the look of terror in Jamison's face. He gets up abruptly. "It's too much for him. I'm gonna leave."

He walks out briskly. To Addison it almost looks like he is running out. "Cams, what was that?" she whispers. "I'm going with him." She kisses Campbell on the cheek and squeezes Jamison's hand. He looks as confused as she feels.

By the time she comes out of the room, Mason is already at the elevator. She limps trying to catch up, her leg feeling stiff and sore. At the elevator door she grabs his hand. As they get in the elevator he looks at her, "I need a few minutes. Can we talk about what happened in there when we get back to your house?" She can tell that he is trying to control the emotion on his face. The terror and fear that are there. Why would Jamison's shock and recognition scare Mason so much?

"Mason, I don't understand what's going on!"

"I said I need some time. I promise I will explain when we get to your place."

They pull into Addison's drive. It is still misty with a little drizzle. A typical Virginia spring day, the type that is followed by an explosion of growth. They park in front of the garden gate. Despite the wet weather, Chandler is jumping behind the gate, excitedly awaiting Addison. He is more anxious than normal, as if he can feel the tension between Mason and Addison. Addison shoos him from the gate. "Move, Chandler." Her harsh voice frightens him, and she is shocked by her own anger. She is angry that Mason made her leave, when she was so happy to see Jamison. She is angry that he isn't telling her why. She has a feeling of foreboding that she can't shake. A feeling that things are about to change irrevocably.

They follow the winding path through the newly sprung daffodils and tulips, their bright, cheerful color such a stark contrast to the day and her mood. He leads her along the path, holding her hand. But now she doesn't feel his strength through their touch, but tension and a cold, icy fear. He leads her to a bench near the back of the garden. They sit facing the trees, shrubs and her mother's little cottage away in the distance. It is a fairytale scene, a scene from a different place and a different world.

"Addie. Angel. I have to tell you something. I was hoping I would never have to. But I know now I have to." He looks at the ground, he won't look at her, but he still holds her hand in his. "The morning Jamison was hit; I had been with you; you were so upset about your injury. Do you remember that? I laid with you throughout the night. We held each other. Then I woke up early because I had to get back to the farm to help my dad. Remember?" Now he finally looks at her, his face is pleading, his eyes are huge pools of dark liquid.

"Yes..." She is afraid of where this is going. She doesn't want to think about it. She doesn't want to hear it.

"I was tired, I was distracted and I was late. I was driving carelessly. I never saw him, he was on the road, not on the path. He wasn't wearing his reflective gear. I didn't even know it was Jamison until it was too late. I was so scared. I reacted with instinct. I drove to Marshall. I changed my tires. I convinced myself it didn't happen. When you wanted to solve the hit and run, I thought maybe we could find someone who could have been there, like I was. That someone else could have hit him as easily as me. I began to convince myself that I didn't do it, that it wasn't my fault. Then I began to hope that Jamison wouldn't remember it was me. But he saw me, the second before I hit him, we saw each other. He knows it was me. I saw that today. I can't lie to you anymore, Addison."

Addison pulls her hand out of his. He makes a move to take it back, but she pulls it so far that he can't grab it without lunging after it. She can't believe what she is hearing. Did he really confess to having hit Jamison? To having lied to her all this time? How could this be the Mason whom she loves, the same man who protects her, cares for Jamison, watches out for Campbell? Could this gentle boy, this kind person be capable of something so horrible? And then mislead her? Help her find a fake culprit? Her brain can barely process it all.

"You lied!" Now she jumps up, "You misled me, you pretended to help me solve the mystery of his accident. For God's sake, you even tried to blame poor Mrs. Anderson. Who are you even? Is there any honesty in you at all? Don't you understand that it was an accident and if you had pulled over, called for help, it would be just that? A horrible, awful accident? That I could have forgiven! But this? This is deceit beyond anything I can imagine!"

"I know. If you could only know how many times I've wished, I could go back and change things."

"Go!" she screams at him. "I don't want to even look at you!"

Mason gets up slowly. He looks at her with pain and regret in his eyes. "I know. I'll go." He turns slowly from her, looks back at her once again, and then he walks along the path, away from her. Chandler follows him with his eyes, looking after him with confusion and back to Addison. He whimpers at her feet. She crouches down, wrapping her arms around him. Alone in the garden, surrounded only by deceit.

What should she do? Should she report him to the police? Does she reveal him in her story? She wanted the biggest story of her life. Well, here it is. Mason has literally and figuratively led her down the garden path. Any faith and trust she has had in him disappears down the path, along with his figure. Even as her trust is annihilated, everything she held true about Mason is false, her heart breaks, because what she felt for him was real. She watches him walk along the path, leaving her alone in the garden. She can't help herself, she loves him. His tall strong frame, his long stride, his dark hair, his gentle touch and kind heart move further and further away from her, leaving her with the decision about what to do about their terrible secret.

The End

Look for the next book in the Addison Erhard Series, *In the Chilling Wind*, coming in 2017.

Acknowledgements

Thank you to Beth Miller for being an incredible editor, not only finding all my misplaced commas, but helping me to develop the characters and storyline. Andrine Strack for being an incredible mother and editor and in believing in my ability to write this novel. Candice Hemlinger for reading my novel and giving constructive feedback and advice. Jessica Kronzer for being my student editor, and lending her perspective for authenticity. Lisa and Nicole McCarthy for reading my novel through all its stages, helping my characters become realistic and having faith in my writing. Kyle McCarthy and Grant Donaldson for reading through my track scenes, talking about what teen track athletes go through and lending those scenes authenticity. Dave McCarthy for providing a summer retreat to write in and cheering me on along the way. Stephanie Evers for talking me through the plot, helping me finish the novel and supporting me. Mary Beth Starkey for reading the story and giving me great feedback and suggestions. Theodore Drescher who read the proofs with me and gave all sorts of excellent editorial advice. Sabrina Drescher for designing the cover to my book and in encouraging me to make this more than just a love story. Willem Drescher for tolerating all my conversations about my book on the way to and from school. Randy Peyton for giving me the time and room to write, early in the morning, late and night and during all his favorite shows.

About the Author

This is Charlotte Peyton's first novel. Charlotte is a Certified Journalism Educator and teaches Journalism, Photojournalism and English in Virginia. She is currently working on a sequel to *Along the Garden Path – In the Chilling Wind.*

Charlotte was born in The Hague, The Netherlands, and was raised in Minneapolis, Minnesota, where she attended Mounds View High School and The University of Minnesota. She currently lives in Virginia, with her husband, three children her dog, Bandit, cat, Scooby and lizard, Humphrey.

Learn more about Charlotte's book at
www.authorcharlottepeyton.com

Book Club Discussion Questions

1. How would you describe Addison? What drives her? Was her portrayal realistic? Can you relate to her?

2. Does Mason seem realistic? How do you think he fits in with the McLean community?

3. Why do you think Mason's parents don't want him to follow in their footsteps?

4. Describe the relationship between Addison and her mother, Elizabeth. How do you think her mother has influenced her career choice and her attraction to Mason?

5. What does Addison learn about herself throughout the book?

6. Do you think Elizabeth Erhard made the correct choice by marrying Derrek despite her concerns? Would you have liked to learn more about Mason's mother?

7. Was the premise of the book interesting? Why or why not? What did you learn about the pressures kids live under?

8. How did the hit-and-run accident change the dynamics of the story, and the relationship between Addison and Mason?

9. Were you surprised by how Mason and Addison approach solving the mystery? Explain why or why not.

10. As you were reading, did you have an idea of who might have hit Jamison?

11. How does the author develop the relationship between Addison and Mason? Is it realistic?

12. Why might the author have chosen to tell the story from third person perspective, rather than first? What are the benefits and drawback?

13. What difference does the structure make in the way you read or understand the book?

14. What main ideas—themes—does the author explore? Consider the title, often a clue to a theme.)

15. How does the author use symbols to reinforce the main ideas?'

16. Did the use of the idiom "Along the Garden Path" make sense? How did the author use the garden as part of the story development and plot?

17. What passages strike you as insightful, even profound? Perhaps a bit of the dialog that's funny or poignant or that encapsulates a character? Maybe there's a particular comment that states the book's thematic concerns?

18. Is the ending satisfying? If so, why? If not, why not...and how would you change it?

19. If you could ask the author a question, what would you ask?

20. Has this novel changed you—broadened your perspective? Have you learned something new or been exposed to different ideas about people or a certain part of the country?

Made in the USA
Charleston, SC
03 February 2017